A
DEADLY
GAME

A DAVID BLAISE MYSTERY

A DEADLY GAME

A DAVID BLAISE MYSTERY

MB DABNEY

Per Bastet

A Deadly Game
A David Blaise Mystery

Published by Per Bastet Publications LLC, P.O. Box 3023 Corydon, IN 47112

Cover by T. Lee Harris

ISBN 978-1-942166-86-3

Available in trade paperback and DRM-free ebook formats

A DEADLY GAME

A DAVID BLAISE MYSTERY

To Ericka and Barbara Michelle, the best two daughters a father could have.

Acknowledgments

First and foremost, I thank Angela, the person in my life who brings out the best in me, despite being the person in my life who has to tolerate the worst, as well. You encourage me and support me in every way. Thank you so much, Sweetheart. I love you.

There are so many who have helped me with inspiration, research, encouragement or with just plain old-fashioned friendship. Among those are: Linda and Hugh Burroughs, Diana Catt, Cynthia Compton, Sharyn Flanagan, Joel Hennessy, Debbie Lawson, Robin Lovelace, Abigail Manning, Melany Martinez, Aliki Megas, Pam Moran, David Norwood, Amicia Ramsey, Patricia Raybon, Steve Terrell, Janis Thornton, Charles Todd, Rohini Townsend, Vivian Wiemelt, the late Darrell Gibson, the members of the Keystone Men's Book Club, and Veronica Foote and the ladies of the book club at the Carmel Lutheran Church. Thank you all.

And, of course, this book would not be possible without the help and guidance of Marian Allen, T. Lee Harris, and Sara Marian at Per Bastet Publications. Thanks for your patience and, above all, for your creativity and talent.

CHAPTER I

"We need to talk."

I knew it was going to be a difficult day as soon as I heard Clara say, "We need to talk." But *that* wasn't the first sign.

I had been dodging my landlord for days and my Mustang was on the fritz. Again.

Last night during a rare Sunday evening dinner alone with my grandmother, I was forced into a long conversation about my sister and her husband. Over perfectly fried chicken — I love drumsticks, by the way, which is why she made them — over perfectly fried chicken, with mashed potatoes and gravy, green beans, homemade rolls, and cherry cobbler for dessert, Grammy Taylor told me in no uncertain terms that I needed to address a situation with my brother-in-law.

Today!

Or at least by tomorrow.

The fact that my sister's marital problems were none of my business — and both Valerie and Stuart would say as much to my face — did nothing to dissuade my grandmother or to influence her command that I act. "You're the oldest male in the family now," she reminded me. "It's your responsibility."

And now this morning, just as Clara was heading out the door to her job at the city transit authority, she said to me, "We need to talk."

Why do they do that? I hate it when a woman says, *"We need to talk"* — or something similar, such as, *"Why don't you. . . ?"* Or, *"When are you going to. . . ?"*

It's never a conversation men are ready to have. Otherwise,

we'd already be doing whatever it is women think we should be doing.

So, as much as I love them, I'll never understand women.

Oh, I can understand their body language and their verbal cues. It's their thinking processes I find difficult to read.

However, it's my job to be able to quickly read people — men and women — and to make decisions based on that understanding. It's essential to my occupation.

My name is David Blaise and I'm a private detective.

"I can't do it now, David," Clara said, walking down the steps from the second floor of her three-story townhouse in the Art Museum area of Philadelphia. The view from her third-floor bedroom looked out over the walls of Girard College, the famed boarding school for poor children. I had my own place — an apartment in West Philadelphia near the University of Pennsylvania. Clara helped me pick it out. But still, I spend most nights in her townhouse on 25th Street, just a few doors south of Poplar Street.

"Look, David," she said, grabbing her winter coat hung on a hook in the entry, "You can't just ignore me until it's convenient for you. This is a relationship . . . a two-way relationship. I need you to act like you're in it."

"I am in it, Clara," I protested with conviction as I helped her on with her coat. "It's just that I work a lot. You know how hard it is. I'm a one-man shop. If I don't do it, it doesn't get done. It all takes so much time and I'm struggling to make ends meet most of the time."

She hung her purse over her shoulder. Then her eyes softened and the muscles all over her body seemed to relax. Clara pulled me close and planted a soft kiss on my left cheek.

"Listen, Boo, we need to talk. Tonight. Just to work out some things. That's all," she said. But as she turned to leave, the stern school mistress attitude returned. "No excuses about work tonight. I mean it. Dinner. Seven-thirty. Tavern on Green.

Don't be late."

And with that, I grabbed my coat and we both headed out the door.

Work wasn't going to be much of a problem. I only had one working case, a snoop job. My client owned a small accounting firm and needed me to investigate whether his partner was stealing. So other than that, I'd spend most of the day looking for another paying client. And while business was currently lean, domestic cases, such as following a philandering spouse or conducting pre-divorce investigations, were my bread-and-butter. I hated the skullduggery nature of it all but it paid the bills.

And such cases never go out-of-season.

Clara's car was parked a half block away. Her job downtown at SEPTA wasn't in the same direction as my office in North Philadelphia, and she didn't have the time to give me a ride. So, I walked to the corner and waited in the cold for a trolley for a ride down to Broad, then took the Broad Street Subway to Erie Avenue in North Philadelphia.

Since it was late February, I didn't dawdle on the one-block journey to my office.

Office is somewhat of an exaggeration. I had a small space in the back of a two-man accounting office that was sandwiched between a hair salon and dentist office on Broad, one of the busiest streets in the city. One of the accountants, Larry Centerton, was both my landlord and, secretly, my client. He was the one who had hired me to quietly investigate his partner, Leslie King. I never had a good handle on what King did because he was rarely in the office.

Neither King nor Centerton were there when I arrived, so I unlocked the front door and headed to the back, where there was a small storage room that was converted into my office. Over in one corner were two large filing cabinets and a load of boxes piled up to the ceiling. Most of it was from the accounting firm.

I had a stiff-back metal chair and a wooden desk that was too large for the limited space. Despite my relative youth — I'm in my early 30s — sitting in the unpadded chair too long hurt my butt and my back. For that reason, and because of the claustrophobic nature of the space, I spent as little time in the office as possible.

Once at my desk, as I was about to start a little administrative work, which I hated, I noticed a note from Larry on my telephone. I reached for it just as the phone rang. Eyeing the note — which only said, "We need to talk." — I answered the call.

"David Blaise Investigations."

"Davey, it's me. Stuart. I need your help," said my brother-in-law.

I didn't say anything at first, unsure of how to proceed. My grandmother wanted me to talk to him about the state of his marriage. Did she also pressure him into calling me?

"This isn't about . . . uh . . . you and Val, is it? Because if it is, I don't want to have anything to do with it. I'm sorry, but she's my sister. I don't want to get involved with your domestic problems," I said, holding the phone speaker close to my mouth so he could clearly hear my intent.

Stuart didn't speak at first, pausing probably to consider what to say.

"No, it's not about Valerie. It's more serious than that," he said, and I immediately sensed he regretted putting it that way. "That's not what I mean. But this is serious, David, and I need some help . . . some investigative help."

There was so much desperation in his voice, I could nearly hear him sweat as he added, "Please."

CHAPTER II

"You levelin' with me, Stuart?"

Stuart Thomas is a real estate owner and developer, and quite a successful one. And Valerie obviously loves him, despite their problems. The attitude of the rest of the family toward the man was, however, more of tolerance than of any genuine affection. And the feeling was mutual. At family gatherings, such as most Sunday night dinners at Grammy Taylor's house, Stuart generally wore his sense of superiority openly.

They met in college; Valerie was still living at home and attending Temple, studying finance; Stuart was across town at Penn, working on his MBA at the Wharton School, specializing in urban planning. Their educations — and wise business decisions afterwards — paid off for both. They got married after college and now live with their two kids (twins) in a large comfortable house in a small comfortable neighborhood in Elkins Park in Montgomery County, less than a mile outside Philadelphia city limits. Their early 20th Century Tudor-style home was designed by famed Philadelphia architect Horace Trumbauer and was once owned by a member of the Gimbel's department store family.

Stuart owned, managed, or developed dozens of commercial and residential properties throughout the area. He specialized in gentrification, particularly in Center City, but also in other parts of the city. That is, aside from Northeast Philadelphia. The Great Northeast, as it is generally called, is still too white, working-class and conservative to easily welcome a smart, young Black businessman from downtown with a swagger in his walk, confidence in his ideas, and the cash to back them up.

Stuart maintained his main office in the heart of the city, on Market Street, less than a mile west of City Hall. Thus, he was highly visible in the city's emerging business community.

My sister Valerie managed the largest Center City branch of the Philadelphia Savings Fund Society, the largest and oldest savings bank in the United States. A family-oriented person by nature, yet also quite ambitious, Val was less well-known than her husband. As such, her ability was something Stuart under-estimated, which was one of his shortcomings.

The truth, however, is that Valerie was a key component to Start's success — personally and professionally. At the bank, she could steer business prospects in his direction, although without revealing any privileged financial information.

Personally charming at times, Stuart could just as likely be rude and difficult. But Valerie softened his edges in social settings, made sure his dress shirts were laundered, his dress pants were crisp and sharply pressed, and insured that jackets weren't too tight if he was gaining weight.

Yet despite Stuart's personal shortcomings, he was a kind and loving father, and seemed to genuinely care about my sister, their differences notwithstanding. It's why I was willing to cut him some slack.

I arrived at mid-morning in the offices of the Stuart Thomas Management and Development Company. The offices were slick, contemporary, and conveyed a *Go Get 'Em* sense that matched Stuart's personality perfectly. His employees were going about their work when I was escorted to his fifth-floor office, where the door to his inner sanctum was open. Stuart was pacing around inside.

And yelling.

"Susan, I don't care what Swanson says. I want those estimates today or he's fired. You tell him that," he said, adding, in a dismissive way, "You can go now."

His secretary, a pretty young white woman in a black skirt and white blouse, hurriedly walked out. Seeing me, she was about to speak but Stuart saw me at the same moment. "Davey, come on in. Susan, shut the door."

Stuart indicated for me to take a seat at the oval conference room table that dominated one end of his office. It offered a wonderful view of the street below. Taking a swig from a Pepsi that was sitting on his desk, he looked at me and said, "You want a soda or something? I know you like Coke, but I don't keep any of that around here."

"Coffee. If you have it," I said.

Stuart rushed to the door and flung it open. I wasn't sure how far away his secretary was but she must have been close because he didn't yell. Or maybe he was just tired of raising his voice.

It was a toss-up.

"Susan, get my brother-in-law here a cup of coffee," he said out the door, before turning back to me. "How do you take it? Cream? Sugar?" Before I had a chance to answer, he turned back to speak outside the office. "Bring both."

He shut the door and walked over to grab his drink sitting on a coaster on his highly polished wooden desk. On a credenza behind the desk were a few knick-knacks of his personal life — pictures of Val and the kids, a picture of him on a sail boat with some business associates or clients, and an elaborate clock I gave him for Christmas years earlier when he had only had a small operation.

Drink in hand, Stuart came over to take a seat close to me. Very close. He was out of sorts. I had never seen him crowd another person's private space to this degree. As loud and commanding as he had been when I entered, he was quiet and nervous when we started to talk.

"Have you read today's paper?" he asked off the bat.

"Uh, no. Not yet. Haven't had the time," I said.

Stuart jumped up as if a hot fire was suddenly lit under his seat and went to his desk, where I could see several copies of both the Inquirer and Daily News. He brought over the Daily News and dropped it on the table in front of me.

"Read the story at the top of page five."

I took the paper and opened it. Stuart walked to the window and stared out until there was a soft knock at the door. He turned just as Susan entered carrying a tray with a mug with the company logo on it, a coaster, a bamboo stir stick, a small packet of creamer, and several packets of sugar. She laid them in front of me without saying a word and I thanked her as she left. Stuart said nothing to her and went back to staring out the window.

The newspaper story had a byline of a staff writer named Georgios Aristidis.

> Police say the body of a North Philadelphia man shot three times in the chest and head was discovered late last night in a house in the Queen Village section of South Philly.
>
> The man was identified as Henry Cummings, 49, of the 1200 block of Thompson Street. He was found on the third floor of a house on Catharine near 5th after nearby residents reported hearing gunshots fired at around 10:30 p.m.
>
> "When officers arrived at the scene, they discovered the body of a black man shot in one of the upstairs bedrooms. He was hit twice in the chest and once in the head," said Lt. Tony Daniels of South Detectives. He went on to say there were no signs of struggle or a motive for the shooting. Nothing seemed missing from the house.
>
> No gun was recovered, he said.
>
> "There was no one else in the residence when police arrived," Daniels added.

Neighbors said they heard shots and called police. But authorities have not found anyone who witnessed seeing someone entering or leaving the property.

"It's such a quiet area. I've lived here my whole life. Never saw anything like it," said 71-year-old Sylvia Woods, who lives next door but who said she was asleep at that hour and didn't hear the shots.

"Now we have that Colored mayor that they elected last year. They'll be taking over the whole city. Might have to move to New Jersey. But not Camden. Too many Hispanics."

Although it could not be immediately confirmed, Cummings reputedly operated a large illegal numbers organization in North Philadelphia. Officials were not sure if that was related to the shooting.

"We're checking on that right now," Daniels said. "It's part of our on-going investigation."

Philadelphia police said the number of murders so far this year is down because of an increased number of officers on the street.

I read quietly as I sipped my coffee. When I finished, I put the paper down and turned to Stuart.

"Okay. What's this about?"

Stuart returned to the conference table, again sitting close to me, leaning with his elbows on his knees. He spoke in a low voice, as if there was some sort of conspiracy.

"That house . . . where the guy was shot and killed . . . that house . . . belongs . . . to me," he said with thoughtful hesitation. But then he noticed how that must have sounded and quickly added, "Not me, personally. It belongs to the company."

"But you own the company, Stuart," I interrupted, though he apparently wasn't listening, as he kept talking.

"We use it as a guest house," he said. "It's a great location. The area's really coming up. Lots going on down there, residential development, retail, restaurants. Lots of stuff. Good area to invest in. That's why we got the house. That and some other properties down there."

I knew the area well. Queen Village. Just a few blocks south of South Street, which is, as the song goes, "The hippest street in town."

I sat back, in part to think, in part just to recover a bit of personal space. Stuart didn't move.

"What's the house used for?"

"Out of town guests, mostly. Clients who like the privacy of a residential property as opposed to a hotel room. And it's there, on those occasions, when we want to take someone down to South Street for the nightlife. But we were thinking of putting it on the market soon," Stuart said.

He stopped, as if to think before he continued. His eyes were on me but not focused on me.

"We also use it, sometimes, for private entertainment purposes of our guests. You know what I mean," he said, now focused on me. "Private, discreet entertainment for very special clients."

I looked at him closely because I caught where he was going. "Was anyone there last night? Anyone being 'entertained' as you put it?"

"No, not last night. But," he said, getting up to walk to his desk. His back was still to me and he hadn't finished whatever he was saying.

"What?" I prodded.

"Nothing," he said without turning back.

I let it go.

"This guy who was killed. How'd he get in? For that matter, how'd the killer get in? Paper says it didn't look like a burglary. Must've had a key," I said.

"I don't know how."

"Did you know this guy, what's his name . . ." I said, picking up the paper, "Henry Cummings?"

"No. Never heard of him before."

I wasn't sure if I believed him. As a person with close political ties to the new W. Wilson Goode administration and connections throughout the area's business community, he knew — or at least heard of — everyone of any importance in the city. But I said, "Then what's the problem, other than a murder happening in a house your company owns?"

Stuart turned to look at me as if I was insane, which may have been accurate. It was an insanely obvious question. But he was hiding something and I needed to press him to find out what.

"I've been in the house. We all have," Stuart said, turning away from me again. "My fingerprints are in there." Stuart was rubbing his pant legs as if to get something sticky off his hands.

"You levelin' with me, Stuart?" I finally said.

"Yes, David. Of course," he said, coming to stand over me at the table.

"Stuart," I said, leaving no doubt of my concern by the tone of my voice.

"I've told you everything. Honest." He sat back down. "But I need your help. We own the house through a shell corporation. It's not . . . on our corporate books."

"What in the world are you doing, Stuart?" I asked.

"Happens all the time. For investment and tax purposes. We get a property, renovate it, up the value and sell it again, taking a nice profit. Everyone in our business does it all the time."

"But no dead bodies are being discovered in anyone else's house."

"I know, I know," he said, rubbing his temples. "If it got out that we own the house, it could really hurt our business."

I was stunned by the statement and by his lack for other concerns.

"A man is found dead and all you're worried about is your business?" I asked. "That's your main concern? Not who killed him?"

"Well, Valerie, too," he said. "Things have been a bit . . . ah . . . strained between us lately. I work a lot of hours. And, well, it's affected things between us."

"I can't get into your personal life with my sister."

"I'm not asking you to," he interjected quickly.

"Then what are you asking me to do, Stuart?"

"I need you to find out why that guy was in my house and who killed him."

"Stuart, I don't know. . . ."

"Please, Davey. I don't know who else I can turn to."

"What about the police? It's what they do. Solve crimes."

Stuart continued as if I hadn't said anything. "I'll pay you for it. We will pay. Whatever it takes. What do you charge for this sort of thing? I don't care. We'll pay it. Just keep it quiet."

It was my turn to get up. I walked around the office, thinking. I wasn't working on much at the moment but I rarely handle serious crimes. I do surveillance work — following people around, and the like — and lots of domestic cases. Generally nothing involving life and death. And I've never had a relative as a client, not even a non-blood relative. Or one I didn't much care for.

I turned back to Stuart, who looked sick with worry. "Okay. I'll look, poke around a bit. But don't expect too much. This isn't my area of expertise."

He got up and in a few short strides was on top of me again. He took my hand and pumped it feverishly.

"Thank you, Davey. I really appreciate everything," he said.

"I'm not promising anything, you know."

"You're a detective. You solve things."

"I just don't want you to get your hopes up," I said, trying to take my hand back. "I'll do what I can, but it might not be much."

"Still, I appreciate it. And we'll help you in your investigation in any way we can," he said, still holding my hand and moving us both toward the door. Once he had what he wanted, the meeting was over. "You tell us what you need and I'll get it for you. No questions asked. And send me the bill directly. I'll handle it personally."

With his left hand, Stuart opened in the door of his office and, still holding my right hand, ushered me out. "This is our private arrangement, okay Davey? Can't mention it to Val, or Grammy Taylor, right?"

"It's business. I'll keep it that way."

He let me go, turning back to his office and shutting the door. He might have been relieved by the situation but I had my doubts. However, for the time being, I would keep those doubts to myself.

~*~

I contemplated my next move as I left Stuart's office. I knew he wasn't giving me the full story. And while police may not have discovered who owned the house, in time they would. And the cops would want more than what Stuart told me and would pressure him harder to get it.

Therefore, I decided I wouldn't go to the police right away. Didn't need them pressuring me on my client's identity. Besides, I doubted they would provide me with much information in exchange. Stuart assured me he'd get me a key to look around the house once it was no longer a crime scene.

I decided as a first step, I'd enlist the help of a private source.

It was too cold for me to walk from Stuart's office on Market down to 16th Street and Lombard and I could take a bus, but I didn't need to. This was a paying gig, and I could bill for expenses.

Bracing against the cold and stepping out onto Market Street, I raised my gloved hand and hailed a cab.

CHAPTER III

"Coulda been seein' somebody he shouldna been seein'."

Randolph Williams — I always love a person with two last names — looked like a newspaper man from the 1930s or '40s. He always wore a dark-colored jacket, white shirt, and a thin dark tie, even if it looked totally out of style. He was of an age when men always wore a hat outside, and his hat of choice was a wool felt fedora, with a thick band. In black, of course. In some bygone era, he'd have a slip of paper in the band that read "Press".

He was thin, smoked a lot and drank even more. From the look of him, I doubted he ever rested or took off his clothes. And if he did ever sleep, I wouldn't be surprised if he kept the hat on when he did.

But Randolph was an institution in the Philadelphia press corps. Everyone, in and out of government, knew him. He had sources everywhere. And though Philadelphia, like most major American cities, was covered from end to end by its white-owned newspapers, Randolph worked at the city's largest black newspaper, The Philadelphia Tribune. He had for decades.

The cab dropped me off at the Tribune's door on South 16th Street. I didn't call ahead and was worried that Randolph might be out. In the lobby, the receptionist called upstairs and, just as I feared, Randolph wasn't in.

"Here's my card," I said, pulling a white and black business card from a jacket pocket inside my overcoat and handing it to the receptionist. "Would you see to it that he gets it? And ask him to call me as soon as he gets in."

She took the card but her reply surprised me.

"There's a bar down on Fifteenth Street. It's called Bart's. . . ."

"Uh, no. It's called Black Bart's," said someone else passing through the lobby.

"He goes there a lot. You'll see it," the receptionist continued. "He's probably there now. Usually is when he's not here."

I thanked her and headed out again.

Randolph was just where she said he might be, on a stool at Black Bart's. He didn't see me approach until I saddled up onto a stool next to him. He held a mostly smoked cigarette in his left hand, his fingertips yellowed from his habit, and a shot glass in the right. He was moving the glass to his lips by the time I caught his notice. Downing the drink and setting the glass on the bar, he extended his bony, weathered hand.

"How ya doin', Blaise? What ya doin' here? You wanna drink?" he said, his grip stronger than one would suspect. His bark was equally strong. "Bart. Another glass for my friend here. And put it on my tab."

A short, stocky white man in a dingy white apron over a short-sleeved shirt waddled over and wiped on the bar in front of me with a wet cloth that probably never got washed. He put a shot glass on the bar and turned back for a bottle of whiskey.

It wasn't top-shelf.

"I need some information," I said, as the bartender poured whatever dark liquid Randolph was drinking into a glass for me, and another for Randolph. He took his neat. I did, too.

"You've come to the right man," the bartender said but didn't move away. Whatever was going to be asked, he wanted to be a part of it. It's why bartenders know so much. They listen and overhear a lot.

I hesitated and Randolph took the cue. "Why don't we go sit over here," he said, pointing to a booth along the wall. If the bartender was upset or offended, he dared not show it.

We took a bowl of nuts with us to the booth.

"You heard about Henry Cummings, I assume," I started.

"Ah, Henry. Shot dead. Yeah, I heard. Not surprised, though," he said, popping a handful of nuts into his mouth.

"Oh? Why?"

"Gambling. He's got the biggest numbers racket in North Philadelphia. Ran it out of a filling station at Caleb and Broad streets in North Philly. Had for years."

I visualized the location in my head. I could see it. "Yes, I know that place. On the west side of the street."

"Exactly."

"What was he doing down in a townhouse in South Philadelphia?"

"God only knows. He had a lot of enemies up north. Probably got tired of them coming after him all the time. Maybe he was looking to move some of his operation, develop more business elsewhere," he said.

Randolph looked at his watch and immediately started easing out of the booth. "Speaking of development, damn, I'm late." He downed the last of his drink and grabbed another handful of nuts, which he started popping into his mouth one at a time. "I forgot. I must cover a news conference in City Hall. I gotta go. But come with me. We can talk on the way."

I wanted to protest, to say I had something clsc to do, but I didn't. I got up, leaving my drink untouched, and we left. Randolph didn't seem to care about the drink. After all, he had a tab.

A blast of cold air hit me in the face as soon as we walked outside. I pulled up the collar of my overcoat onto my neck. Randolph, however, only wore a black suit jacket and didn't seem to mind the temperature, which was just below freezing.

"Aren't you cold?" I asked Randolph as we stepped up our pace.

"I got warm blood," he replied.

My guess was the heavy drinking fortified his mind and numbed his senses to the temperature. But Jack Frost could wreak havoc on exposed skin. I hoped Randolph remembered that, despite his bravado.

We headed north on 15th and I silently thanked the gods that City Hall was only three blocks away. "I'm not a reporter. I can't get into this thing, you know."

"Oh, of course you can. Nobody knows you aren't a writer and nobody's gonna ask. Just stick close to me. When it starts, just stand near the back and don't talk." Randolph reached into his inside jacket pocket and pulled out a spiral reporter's notebook and handed it to me. "I always carry an extra, just in case I need a spare."

"Thanks," I said, accepting the gift.

"Henry was violent when he needed to be," Randolph said, his gloveless hands stuffed deep into his coat pockets. He must have done that so many times the edges in the well-worn jacket were beginning to rip. "They called him 'The Hatchet Man' because of the way he got rid of his rivals. I'm surprised someone got him like that."

"You think it was someone gunning for his operation . . . sorry for the pun?" I said.

"Could've been, but the location doesn't seem right. They could've shot him in North Philly. Much more accessible there, I'd think," Randolph said, dropping several more nuts into his mouth as we walked, crossing Chestnut Street. "Sounds more personal to me this way. He was married but he really liked the ladies. Got out a lot. Coulda been seein' somebody he shouldna been seein'."

That made some sense, given how Stuart said the house was sometimes used.

"We print the numbers, you know, the daily numbers. Just like the Pennsylvania lottery numbers. We put the street numbers in the paper. I get them every day," he said without the slightest hint of the impropriety of doing so.

We got to City Hall, a massive masonry structure that housed all three branches of Philadelphia city and county government, and we walked around to enter the building from the east side. Our destination was on the second floor.

The Mayor's Reception Room is one of the most ornate in City Hall. Greek columns flank its door, a massive chandelier hangs from the ceiling and pictures of former mayors dominate one wall. A podium, with Philadelphia's seal on the front, was set up with its back to a large ornamental fireplace. Chairs faced the podium as reporters and cameramen prepared for the mayor and other city officials to enter.

"What's this about?" I whispered in Randolph's ear as he placed a tape recorder on the podium to catch what was about to be said.

"Supposedly something about economic development. There's a press release over on the table near the door. Get one for me, too," he said.

I got two copies of the release, found a seat, and started reading just as Mayor Goode entered, followed by a gaggle of other officials. I don't closely follow local government and I didn't recognize anyone in the group. And while Goode was the shortest of the lot, his commanding attitude left no doubt that he was the one in charge.

The reporters settled into chairs, and the cameramen and photographers took their positions. "Down in front," one photographer yelled to a couple of reporters just as Goode started to speak.

"Thank you for coming. I am pleased today to announce a multi-million-dollar economic development plan for Penn's Landing that will create jobs, expand retail space, and lure more businesses to the area," Goode said. "This is a promise I outlined in my election campaign and it's a promise I intend to keep. To explain more, here is my economic development director, Allison Charles."

From behind the mayor, a tall, attractive Black woman stepped forward. I had never seen or heard of her before because she would be hard to forget. Unlike all the other city officials, who were all decked out as if from a Brooks Brothers store catalog, Charles wore a conservative Navy blue jacket, a straight gray skirt with a periwinkle blue blouse, and pearls. She was striking. And in heels, she towered over Goode.

Looking directly into the television cameras and virtually ignoring the reporters up front, Charles spoke calmly and confidently about a plan that would rejuvenate Penn's Landing and serve as a launching pad for further development throughout the city. I was amazed at her poise as she answered occasionally pointed questions from reporters after she spoke.

Allison Charles was one cool character.

"Are all press conferences that boring?" I asked Randolph as we headed down the stairs to the street twenty minutes later.

"Some," was his only reply.

"And who was that woman? The economic development woman?" I asked as we walked west through the City Hall courtyard toward 15th.

"Allison Charles. She's new, of course, but she was in charge of economic development during the mayor's election campaign. Not from Philly. From somewhere out west. But she went to Wharton and then stayed. Knows everything there is to know about urban redevelopment, I'm told. I don't personally know her, though. Haven't had much opportunity to cover her."

When we reached the street, I made an excuse, saying I had work. Randolph turned south and headed back toward the Tribune — or the bar. I headed down toward the subway and back up to my office.

CHAPTER IV

I doubted it was the police but that was of little comfort.

I knew my landlord, Larry Centerton, was in his office before I arrived because I saw his car in the parking lot across the street. I contemplated just passing by but knew I'd have to talk to him eventually. Might as well get it over with.

Centerton, a man who tipped the scales at 350 pounds if he weighed an ounce, was alone in his nicely appointed office and apparently working on a tax return at his desk, which was a mess of papers. I couldn't imagine how he ever got anything done. It was the reason I had his partner, Leslie King, doing my taxes. Centerton might lose something important in his mountain of debris.

"Larry," I started, pulling up a chair, "I know I'm a little late with the rent but it's been a slow month, with the cold and all."

He addressed me over the glasses perched on the bridge of his nose. "You said that last month."

"And I paid you."

"Late," he added, grabbing a stack of papers as he stared me down.

"Yes, but I paid. In full. You know I'm good for it."

He took off his glasses, laying them on the tax return he was doing, and pushed back in his chair, resting his folded hands on his big belly.

"What progress have you made on my case?"

"I have followed him several nights and nothing out of the ordinary happened. Goes downtown, generally eats alone and has a drink at a hotel bar on Seventeenth Street, and then heads to his house over near Wyomissing."

Centerton pulled a handkerchief from his pocket that looked like it had seen better days. Reaching for his glasses, he fogged them with his breath and wiped the lenses, never taking his eyes off me.

"I know he's stealing money. And I know I'll prove it. I just need you to keep an eye on him until I do, just in case he does something strange," Centerton said.

You're the strange one, I thought. "How much longer do you want him under surveillance?"

He put the glasses on and stared into a space somewhere behind and above my head. It was a long time before he replied.

"I'm going to confront him before it gets worse, probably early next week," Centerton said. "He must think me a fool but I won't tolerate this much longer."

"No doubt," I said, although I did have my doubts.

"Keep an eye on him 'til next week," he said, adding, "We'll see about your rent after that."

I nodded and started to push myself out of my chair when he stopped me. He had a silly grin on his face; an expression I recognized. He was going to venture into something gossipy or sexual. Or both.

"You still seeing that girlfriend of yours? She's One Fine Mama. Uh, uh, uh," he said, shaking his head, his grin widening to that of a Cheshire cat. "If you ain't taking care of her . . . and you know what I mean. Hittin' that thang . . . you let me know. I'll hit it and take care of it good."

Before I could totally object — or just beat the shit out of him — the telephone rang in my office. The god of Abraham, Isaac and Moses just saved his life, although he didn't know it.

Without saying a word, I rose and went to answer the

phone.

"David Blaise Investigations."

"Blaise, this is Bob over at Bob's Automotive. Your Mustang's done and ready for pick-up."

It was a relief to know but I squinted my eyes shut before I asked the question. "What's the damage? The cost?"

"Not too bad. Three fifty-seven, eighty-nine. That's taxes and everything."

I exhaled and once again thanked the god of Abraham, Isaac and Moses. It was more than I wanted to pay but less than I expected. It would leave me with less than two hundred dollars in the bank and with the rent due on my apartment in less than two weeks. But I'd be able to eat. Plus I still had a retainer for doing occasional security work for SEPTA. And, starting today with Stuart, I had another cash-paying client. I might just survive.

"I'll be up to get it in an hour."

It was going on three in the afternoon and Bob's was on 22nd Street south of Walnut in Center City. I had just enough time to stop by Stuart's office to get a key to the house in Queen Village, pick up the car and conduct a little investigation before dark. Before dark was essential.

And it would allow me just enough time to meet Clara for dinner at seven-thirty.

~*~

I joined the Navy after I graduated from Temple University and served in an intelligence unit in Italy. I enjoyed it. However, sadly, both my parents died during my tour of duty, which increased my homesickness, and after four years in the service, I grew disillusioned. Despite the promise of a nice bonus if I re-upped, I left the Navy and headed home, jobless but with some money in my pocket.

I stayed with my grandmother in North Philadelphia for a month as I got settled. On the second day I was home, I visited a Ford dealer in Northeast Philadelphia off Cottman Boulevard and bought a brand new, 1976 Mustang on the spot. It was white, with a thin red stripe running along the side. AM/FM radio, thin white wall tires, and a four-speed manual transmission. To this day, I don't understand why anyone but a very old person would want anything but a manual transmission.

I financed it for thirty-six months and it ran reasonably well for nearly five years due to good upkeep and regular maintenance. But now, eight years out, maintenance and upkeep were becoming more and more costly. And while I'd like to trade it in for something newer, it wasn't in my budget. Not now.

Maybe next year.

From Bob's, I drove the Mustang down South Street to 4th Street and hung a right. At Catharine, I took another right and slowly drove up the street. My Navy intelligence training came in handy almost immediately. I spotted the unmarked police car with two officers inside sitting directly in front of the house where the murder occurred. It was in the middle of the block and I kept going, not even slowing down. There were no other police cars, which was a good sign.

I drove up to 6th and took a left and parked in the first space I could find, which was more than a block away. Heading back on foot in the direction of the house on Catharine but on the adjacent street, I stopped at 5th and looked in both directions for any police presence. Nothing.

Fingering the house keys in my coat pocket, I walked up a narrow alleyway that ran behind the homes, stopping directly behind the house of the murder scene. I looked both ways again and then opened the gate to the six-foot, wooden privacy fence and stepped onto a well-kept patio. I used a key to turn off the alarm on the panel beside the door, unlocked the door and entered. I didn't hear a sound inside. I was alone.

It was still light outside but I wouldn't have turned on a light anyway. Didn't want to alert the officers outside.

The kitchen surprised me. It was spotless, of course. I expected the look to be more like Sears than like Scandinavian Design. It was all black and white cabinets with beveled glass fronts and expensive silver handles. The counter looked like marble. Italian tile graced the floor.

The white dishes were high-end designer, and the pots and pans hung from hooks attached to a circular metal holder that itself was attached to the ceiling. The sugar and flour canisters were full, the spice rack held a greater variety of spices than I thought existed, and the walk-in pantry was full of designer foods.

This was the kitchen of someone who wanted the best things money could buy and loved to cook. And clearly was often used.

Easing myself down the hallway toward the front room, I checked to make sure the police outside could not see me. I was impressed by the artwork, which leaned toward the modern. But I didn't linger to admire the pieces, not even the ones hung on the wall leading to the next floor. I didn't make a sound on the hardwood as I made my way up the steps. The police might not notice me but the nosy neighbor next door might.

I was surprised again on the second floor. I expected a display of the same expensive tastes that dominated the downstairs but the second floor was quite ordinary, except for the runner on the floor from one end of the house to the other. There was a bathroom and three bedrooms — two small bedrooms in the rear and a large one in the front. I looked inside but didn't go in, not wanting to get too close to the window. There was nothing out of the ordinary in any of the rooms. In fact, they didn't look like they had been used in quite a while.

I ventured up to the top floor, which had only a bedroom but it was impressive. The floor was a polished hardwood, and a thick Persian rug covered the floor near the bed. More art graced the walls, which were a muted, pale, calming gray color. A large mirror hung on the wall over an elaborate mantle that held two small vases with fresh-cut flowers on either end.

Steering clear of the windows, which faced the street below, I went to the king-sized bed. It had silk sheets under a puffy white comforter. Sitting and then bouncing on the bed, I discovered it to be quite firm. Good for sleeping. Good for sex, too, I imagined.

Though homey, the room, like most of the upper part of the house, lacked a certain personal touch. Someone could stay there but no one probably lived there. There were no personal pictures or memorabilia anywhere, though the closet held a few items of clothing, both male and female, all carefully hung on hangers.

The woman was tall, or at least taller than Clara or my sister Valerie, the two females I know best, and her clothing was interesting and decidedly expensive because I recognized some of the labels for clothes I had seen in Clara's fashion magazines — names like Halston and Calvin Klein. I don't know who Bill Blass is but judging from the label in the black evening gown in the closet, he's hot stuff. It's hard for me to imagine who would wear such a dress or to where.

But I didn't have time to contemplate such matters. The digital on the nightstand showed it was 4:54. It would be dark soon so I had to hurry.

I entered the bathroom next to the bedroom and looked around. A silk robe with a flowery pattern, clearly designed for a female, hung on a hook behind the door. The towels were a pale yellow, a color a woman might fancy, and were thick and heavy. And expensive. They went well with the walls, which were covered in a fancy wallpaper with blue as the dominant color.

Taking out a handkerchief so as not to leave fingerprints, I checked the cabinets. There were a few items of personal necessity — toothbrushes, paste, mouthwash, shavers and razor blades, deodorant — but one bottle caught my attention. I had seen a bottle like that before and it contained a men's fragrance. The bottle was half empty. Its owner used it often.

Opening the top, I took a whiff and my head snapped back. I knew that scent, though it was both rare and expensive. Valerie showed it to me three months earlier after a Christmas shopping trip to New York. Though clearly a woman used this bedroom and bathroom often, so too, apparently, did my brother-in-law.

Putting the cologne bottle back in its place and closing the cabinet door, I went back into the bedroom and plopped down on the bed to think. I wasn't sure how long I sat but the implications of what I now suspected were enormous.

Suddenly, I heard someone in the house, though they were trying to be as quiet as me.

I got up and looked around, trying to decide what to do and where to go. They sounded like they were in the front of the house and could be headed upstairs. I doubted it was the police, because they had no reason to keep quiet, but that was of little comfort. Whoever it was must have gotten into the house the same way I got in. I quickly ran over several things in my mind, starting with: Did I touch anything without using a handkerchief?

I left the bedroom and inched down a short hallway to a door that led to stairs up to a rooftop deck. Listening quietly and hoping my beating heart didn't give me away, I hid behind the door as someone tip-toed up to the third floor. The heels of their shoes made a distinctive sound on the hardwood tread of the steps.

I was tempted to leave the door open a little but opted to completely close it by the time the intruder reached the third floor. I waited, half-expecting them to come in my direction but when they didn't, I cracked open the door to see who it was. I instantly recognized those shoes, those long legs, that Navy blue jacket and the periwinkle blue silk blouse with the collar over the back collar of her jacket.

It was Allison Charles.

CHAPTER V

"We still need to talk. . . . "

I have always enjoyed Tavern on Green, an American eatery at Green and 21st streets in the Fairmount section, but that's not why I got there fifteen minutes early. The fact was, I don't even remember the drive. My mind was somewhere else.

I was seated immediately at a table near the window. Without my having to ask, a waitress, who recognized me from our numerous visits, brought me a soda and one glass of water. And I just sat, my fingers laced together, my mind in thought.

The implication was that Stuart was having an affair with Allison Charles. And if that wasn't enough, there was the possibility that he could have killed Henry Cummings, or knew the "someone" who did. Either way, he lied to me. To my face.

I realized I was jumping to conclusions but regardless, this certainly could throw a wrench into family dinners.

A dead man was found in the house, in the bedroom, where Stuart was likely carrying on a secret relationship with a city official who also couldn't afford for their relationship to become publicly known. He was a property owner and real estate developer. She was the head of urban development in the city. Beyond the moral implications on both the personal and professional levels, the conflict of interest was abundantly apparent.

And was Cummings also sleeping with Allison Charles? Was murder the result of some sort of love triangle?

What was I to do? Confront my brother-in-law? No, I

couldn't do that, not just yet, not without more facts. Then later? Not at all? And what about my sister, Valerie? Should I mention this to her, and possibly destroy her family?

"You're early, Boo," Clara said, approaching the table a few minutes before seven-thirty. Preoccupied, I didn't see her coming. I rose and kissed her cheek before she pulled up a chair and sat. "Given your mood this morning, I half-expected you to be late."

Hanging her coat over the back of her chair, Clara had changed out of her work clothes and was wearing jeans and a fashionable red sweater I gave her for Christmas weeks earlier. The waitress arrived before I had a chance to compliment Clara on how good she looked.

"Hey, Sheree, I think I'll just have a glass of white wine for starters. And I see you've already brought my water," Clara said to the waitress. Across the table, she added, "Aren't you going to have any wine, David?"

"No, I'm good for now."

Clara was a deputy chief of security at the city transit authority, handling all the security on the subways and light rail lines. We met while I was working on the SEPTA police force but we didn't start dating until after I left the force to start my own detective agency. We kept our relationship secret from her job, although she was able, from time-to-time, to steer some security contract work my way.

But I wanted to avoid talking about what was on my mind. I needed to move things in a different direction.

I employed a tactic I learned from my first commander in the Navy. It was especially useful when talking about sports but could be successfully adapted for other subjects. The commander knew very little about most sports but was considered by some as a great sports conversationalist, perhaps even an expert. The key was knowing what sports teams were in the city you're in, and who was playing during that time of year. In conversation, start by saying, "Hey, how 'bout 'em Phillies?" or "How 'bout 'em Sixers?"

If it was baseball season and the person you were talking to didn't care anything about the team or the sport, you'd be off the hook but would probably have to find another subject.

However, if they cared about, say, baseball and particularly if they loved the Phillies, they would totally carry the conversation and do all the heavy lifting. All you had to do was occasionally say, 'Yeah, that's right," and nod your head in agreement with whatever they said. You wouldn't have to know a thing about Mike Schmidt.

The commander used it successfully in the many cities where he was deployed.

Just after we ordered food — Clara had a chicken stir fry and I a mushroom cheeseburger — I started with, "Hey, how's your day?"

She took the bait.

"We got that pickpocket today in the Broad Street line in the Walnut-Locust station. You know the guy. Freddie," she said. "Caught his ass red-handed. Sent him right downtown. But I betcha he'll be out by tonight or tomorrow morning."

I nodded and added, "Yeah, that's right," where appropriate.

We charged on through dinner, and her second glass of wine, without my having to make much conversation. I thought I was home free and considered myself fortunate.

I was wrong on both counts.

"What's wrong, Davey? You haven't said a word all evening," she said, putting down her fork and resting her elbows on the table.

"I'm good, Clara," I responded.

"David," she said, leaving no question that I was caught, "I know something's wrong. What is it? You got your car back? How much was it?"

"Just over three-fifty. I had it."

"And you took care of the rent at your *office?*" Clara never liked my office arrangement. She especially hated Centerton, with good reason.

"It's worked out. I talked to Larry. We're cool."

"Then what is it, David?" she continued to press, holding her wine glass ready to take another sip.

I stroked my non-existent beard and stalled, considering how much to tell her. In the end, I knew I'd have to tell her something, although none of the particulars. I sat back in my chair and she put down her glass and waited.

"I got this new client today who wanted me to look into this situation. It's proving to be more complicated than I originally thought," I said.

She leaned forward. If not for the table, we might have touched. "You can't tell me who it is, can you?" she said in a low voice.

"No. Can't do that."

"What's it about? Can I help?"

I opened my mouth to answer but nothing came out. My brain stopped the words before I was even conscious of the effort. There was something she could do. Setting my own elbows on the table on either side of the plates that hadn't been cleared yet, I made a critical decision.

"Huh, yeah. I think you can help," I said, pausing again. She waited, letting me reach for her. "You're close with some of the cops downtown. You work together. I need something they probably won't give me."

Clara pulled back but kept eye contact, although she managed to grab the wine. I almost had to pull the words out of her before she said, "Whadda you need?"

"There was a man found murdered last night down on Catharine, in Queen Village. Name was Henry Cummings."

"I read about it this morning. He was shot."

"Several times. Yes, that's the one." I stopped and gauged how to move forward. I decided my only option was to jump straight in.

"I need to see a copy of the police report of the shooting."

"You doing a murder investigation, David? This is a big leap . . . a seriously big leap . . . from what you normally do. Who is this client of yours?"

"You know I can't tell you who my client is but no, I'm not doing a murder investigation," I said, lying.

Clara ran her hand through her hair on the right side. I knew the gesture. She was thinking, juggling the conflicting demands of her own professionalism against helping me with a case. I wasn't sure which way she would fall.

"You getting in over your head? Please tell me you aren't in over your head."

"I'm not in over my head." Another lie. Perhaps. I wasn't quite sure yet. Time would tell, hopefully before it was too late. But I also knew it was something I had to pursue.

The waitress came to clear the table, eliminating, for the moment, the need for me to answer a question any more mundane than whether to have dessert. I said no.

"Key lime pie," Clara said, although I don't think she heard herself say it.

Once the waitress was gone, the attention was back on me. "I just need to see the police report. Please," I said.

"Okay. In the morning, I'll call someone down at the Roundhouse and see what I can do. I know a couple people who owe me," she said.

"Thanks, Clara. I appreciate it."

She then returned the conversation to what she always wanted. "We still need to talk about us and we haven't done that yet," Clara said. "We need to see where we're going."

I nodded yes as the pie arrived. "I think we're good right now."

"What do you mean by 'we're good'?" she jumped in. "And where do you think that will take us?"

"I'm not really sure," I started, hoping to find the right words and quietly praying that it would be enough. "But I know I don't want to lose you."

It was just enough.

~*~

We spent the night, for once, in my apartment on Locust near the Penn campus in West Philadelphia. Clara knew a realtor and together they helped me find the place two years ago.

When I got the apartment, it was as far away from my family in North Philadelphia as I thought was possible without moving out of town. It was a nice, small building with four apartments, two on each of two floors. I was on the second floor and the landlord, a sweet older woman named Mrs. Findley, lived in one of the apartments on the first floor. I wasn't sure if Mrs. Findley had a first name or was just born that way.

Clara and I made love, of course, but my mind wasn't in the room as we did it. And if she noticed, she didn't say so. Clara cuddled me tighter than normal afterwards until she went to sleep. Sometime after two in the morning, I eased out of bed and stood over her, staring down and listening to her breathing.

I didn't know where our relationship was going, but I also couldn't think about it now. I reached down to the floor for the pajama bottoms I kicked off before we made love. I walked into my living room and sat in the dark and thought. It was shortly after five o'clock before I got back into bed.

CHAPTER VI

***"Against my better judgment . . . I'm going to help you.
Don't make me regret the decision."***

"I talked to a chief inspector this morning down at the Roundhouse. His name is Larson. Daniel Larson," Clara said over the telephone. I was in my office, barely awake, trying to handle some paperwork and to plot out my next move. I hadn't gotten nearly enough sleep but still got to the office around nine.

"He's expecting your call but he's gonna want you to come down there to see the report. He didn't tell me anything but apparently there are details that aren't being released to the public," Clara said.

"Thanks. Give me the number and I'll call right away," I said, jotting it down.

"Boo, this is a big favor, you know." There was a pause. I waited for what was coming next but I got the feeling she decided against saying more. "Just be careful."

I reassured her and thanked her again before I hung up. The next number I dialed was to Chief Inspector Daniel Larson.

~*~

Most Philadelphia city offices were in the nearly century-old City Hall, once the tallest building in Pennsylvania and still the tallest masonry building in the world. But the Police Department headquarters were in a circular building appropriately called the Roundhouse and located more than a mile from City Hall at 8th and Race streets. The building was surrounded by an eight-foot wall, and had narrow windows all around, giving the impression of a fortress with no unwanted people getting in and certainly no one getting out.

Chief Inspector Larson's office was on the third floor, sandwiched between stairs to lower floors and a dark room with people sitting in front of computer consoles with glaring screens. Telephones were attached to the right side of the consoles.

I was escorted from the first floor up to Larson's office and he rose from behind his desk as I entered. He was a dark-skinned man in his fifties, thin-waisted and physically fit. He wore dark pants and a white shirt more crisply pressed than any shirt I had ever seen. The chief inspector's insignia — a golden eagle with its wings outstretched and a cluster of arrows in its talons — was visible on his epaulets.

Larson stretched out his hand as I approached his desk. His handshake was firm. This was a man in command and he made sure you knew it. "Inspector Larson," was all he said, indicating for me to sit in the chair in front of his desk.

"I'm David Blaise. And thanks for seeing me, Chief Inspector."

He didn't say it was a pleasure to see me but charged straight in the subject at hand.

"Clara Lewis over at SEPTA says you want to see the official police report on that fatal shooting over in Queen Village. For what purpose?" he said with a seriousness that undoubtedly reflected a man who didn't suffer fools easily.

I was expecting the question but still didn't have a really good answer for it. "I'm just looking into some things for a client." I hope I didn't sound too weak.

"Who might that be?"

"I can't really divulge that information."

"Uh, I see," he said, leaning back in his chair and settling a stare on me that bored a hole in my head. "How is this client involved in this case?"

"I can't say that, either." I kept my hands on my legs to keep them from shaking in front of him.

"If you or your client are in any way involved in this case, then I need to know. And if you are withholding information concerning this murder or in any way hinder the investigation, let me assure you of this: We will pull your investigator's license, arrest you and lock you up," he said, sternly adding, "You won't know what hit you."

I had no doubt of his seriousness. The man hadn't smiled or relaxed once since I entered his office.

"That's not going to happen, sir, I promise you. If I find out anything helpful to the police, I will call you immediately and let you know," I said, fidgeting in my chair and hoping he didn't notice.

Not taking his eyes off me, Larson cracked his knuckles. "Against my better judgment and as a personal favor to Clara, I'm going to help you. Don't make me regret the decision."

With that, he picked up a pad and pen from his desk and wrote down a name and telephone number. "This is the name of the officer handling the investigation into this case. Go see him and he will provide the police report."

I thanked Larson, took the note, and escaped his office as quickly as I could.

Once outside, I found a payphone and called the number on the note. After introducing myself to Detective John Thompson of South Detectives, I arranged to head down to see him.

Thompson's office was in a squat building on the southside. Ushering me to his desk in an open room with lots of desks, Thompson, who was friendly and relaxed, was just the opposite of tightly-wound Larson. After my tense encounter with the chief inspector, this was unexpected, though welcomed.

After the introductions, he reached into a file and pulled out the police report I requested.

"This is it," he said. "Most of it has already been reported in the papers and on TV."

I absently agreed with him as I read.

The first police call came in at 10:21 that night and police arrived seven minutes later. Entering the property, they found the deceased in the bedroom on the third floor. He was naked except for a red necktie. He was shot three times in the chest and head with a small caliber gun. Thirty-eight caliber slugs were pulled from the body.

The deceased was named Henry Cummings.

An autopsy revealed that while the gunshots killed him, he was probably unconscious at the time, having been choked by the necktie, perhaps while engaged in a sex act. Nothing was missing in his clothes — his wallet, ID and cash were found — and there did not appear to be a struggle. Nothing was missing in the home as far as the police could determine. There was no violent entry, no broken windows or doors, and no fingerprints on the body or in the room. Everything was wiped clean.

There were no motives or suspects in the case, and the investigation was on-going.

"What's your interest in this case, Mr. Blaise?" Thompson asked when I finished reading.

"Just looking into things."

Another detective in street clothes came up and took a nearby seat. He was younger and thinner than Thompson, and with a more serious facial expression, as if there was little sunshine in his life. He eyed me with caution.

According to a nameplate on the desk where he sat, his last name was O'Donnell. Irish, though his slight olive complexion made him appear as if his ancestry was more southern European.

"Don't get in our way," O'Donnell said without introduction.

Why do they keep saying that? I'm aware of it, I thought.

Thompson looked between us and then made a quick introduction. The newly arrived officer was Johnny O'Donnell, who went about arranging paperwork on his desk as if I wasn't there, though I was sure he was listening closely.

"Were the bullets matched to a particular gun or to a previous crime?" I asked them both.

"Nothing's surfaced so far. But we're still looking," Thompson said.

"I heard Cummings was involved in illegal gambling in North Philadelphia. Is there any connection to that?" I asked.

Thompson scratched the back of his head but it was O'Donnell who answered. "We're looking into that, too. Nothing so far but it's a real possibility. We know some others in the numbers racket up there have disappeared recently without a trace. This could be part of that," he said, sounding irritated.

"But Cummings was killed in South Philadelphia, a bit away from his bailiwick," I countered.

"We are checking into all of that, too," O'Donnell said. More irritation.

"Can I have a copy of the report?" I asked.

The question must have surprised O'Donnell because he shot a look at his partner as he quickly answered, "No."

Time seemed to stand still before Thompson, clearly the senior of the two, spoke. "Normally, no," he said, looking at O'Donnell, who said nothing more, then returned his gaze to me. "But I was instructed to provide you with whatever you needed. Within reason, of course. Let me make you a copy."

O'Donnell didn't look happy but he kept any comments to himself.

"Thanks," I said, getting up and reaching for two business cards in my jacket pocket. "If I hear anything, I'll call."

O'Donnell took the card without glancing at it. Thompson — the good one in this good cop/bad cop scenario — just smiled and went to make copies.

~*~

I needed to find out anything about the handgun used in the crime. However, that was difficult because state law prohibits any law enforcement entity in the Commonwealth from keeping track of gun licenses. However, the state police did keep track of gun purchase permits.

I would start there but first decided to drive uptown to see Randolph again. He was in his office when I arrived and looked exactly as he did a day earlier. Reaching for his hat sitting on his desk next to his computer, Randolph said, "It's time for a smoke," and we walked back outside and stood in front of the Tribune building.

I remained upwind as Randolph puffed away, blue smoke twirling in the wind and disappearing.

"Tell me about Allison Charles," I said.

"I told you about her yesterday. What more do you need to know?"

"Is she married? Where does she live? What part of town?" I started. "Damn, it's cold out today." I patted my arms to keep warm.

"Not married. You lookin' for a new girlfriend?" he said, smiling at my discomfort. "Bit out of your league, I'd say."

"Not looking for a new girlfriend. Dealing with the one I've got is hard enough. What else you got on Allison Charles?"

Shifting his weight and moving about slightly to increase circulation, Randolph continued, "Let me see. Not married. No relationship that I've heard of. Has a townhouse in Fairmount, near Twenty-sixth Street."

"Where is she from?"

"Not sure but she graduated at the top of her class at Wharton. Specializes in urban planning. Worked for the

DRPA for five years doing economic development along the river before joining the Goode campaign a year ago. Has close friends in the administration and allies in City Council. She's very ambitious and Goode has a lot of confidence in her."

"DRPA? "

Randolph looked at me like I had just insulted his mother.

"The Delaware River Port Authority. They own four bridges over the Delaware River between Jersey and Pennsylvania. With all those cars crossing over every day and all those tolls, it's a cash cow. The DPRA is awash in money. It defines patronage in Philadelphia and South Jersey. You should know that," he scolded.

I ignored the verbal spanking. He was a source of information. Not knowing something was why I came to him. "So I guess she's really plugged in."

"All economic development in the city has to go through her first," he said.

"Friends and enemies?"

"Besides the mayor, hard to say who her friends are, but she's got 'em. And on City Council, too. John Street, who's angling to be Council president one day, is a supporter. As for enemies, too many to count. But she's smart, though, and is keeping them at bay."

"Would it be hard for me to get a meeting with her?"

"For you? I can't see why she'd take it," he said.

"But with some help . . . your help . . . could it be arranged?"

Randolph dropped the butt of his filter-less cigarette to the ground and stepped on it. "Let me know when and I'll see what I can do. I have someone who owes me a favor and who's close to someone in her office. I can probably get you on her calendar. But after that, you're on your own."

With that, he went back inside to work.

CHAPTER VII

An uncomfortable truth

Raymond Dawson was my best friend at Ben Franklin High School, in part because he had easy access to a car. We were quite a pair. I was tall, thin, and intensely insecure around girls. Ray was no more than five-foot-seven — in platform shoes — but charming in a way girls loved and guys respected. He was the leader and I was his sidekick. We'd cruise the streets in search of the best house parties with good dance music and cute girls, or for the best hamburger joints, though his father's promise of the pain of death meant we rarely ventured out of North Philadelphia.

By that time, the school was predominantly Black, and Ray and I joined a student-led effort to rename the school after Malcolm X. The effort failed, of course, though even now, we still refer to our alma mater by that name.

My family barely had the money for my college tuition, so I lived at home when I entered Temple. But Ray's dad coughed up the money to get Ray into a dorm, where his magnetic personality flourished. His dorm room was always full of other students, more often than not of the female variety, where much partying occurred and occasionally some studying was done. He majored in business — with a minor in his true love, dance — and I in political science.

We joined Omega Psi Phi during our sophomore year, and our frat names were a reasonable reflection of the two young men whom we were. He was Mad Dog. I was Snoopy Dog.

Ray's dance skills were so legendary, he choreographed our fraternity's line dance.

Our heady idealism was in full bloom during those early college years but reality smacked us head-on in the spring of our senior year. I won acceptance to Penn law school, but my pocketbook was no fuller than it was four years earlier. And thus, I saw my only way out of North Philadelphia was with the Navy, a direction to which Ray vehemently objected.

"Snoopy, you'd be selling out to The Man," he said. We were having a burger and a drink at our favorite joint on Broad Street, an easy walking distance a few blocks north of the main Temple campus. "It's just what The Man wants. You can't do that, Snoop. Don't be a sellout."

Given our years of social activism, the suggestion that I'd be a sellout stung. I tried to overlook it.

"I gotta get out of here. I can't take it any longer," I said. "Besides, once I finish with the Navy, I can still attend law school, and the GI Bill would pay for it. I can still change the world."

"N'all, man. That ain't happenin'. You're giving up your dreams. Everything you've wanted and have worked for," Ray said as he pushed back his chair to get up, leaving half his food.

I stopped him, if only briefly.

"It's different for you, M-D. You've got family to help you while you're in grad school," I said, stating an obvious truth, though later I regretted saying it. "I don't have that option."

My argument left Ray unmoved. By the time we graduated, and I shipped off to the Navy, we were barely speaking.

We did hang out sometimes when I was in town on leave, but physical distance wasn't the only thing that divided us. Our lives were heading in different directions. I was an intelligence officer stationed in Italy. He went to grad school in New Jersey and afterwards, he was the hotshot young business exec with a fresh MBA working at a Jersey-based retail store, where many of the managers were women and all of them were anxious to please him.

It was not, however, the career in dance that he envisioned.

After I left the Navy, we settled into a comfortable acquaintanceship that required little from us other than simple greetings on birthdays and holidays, or at the occasional fraternity party, even though we lived in the same city.

So, imagine my surprise one evening when, as I enjoyed a beer and pizza after a long day of working on my brother-in-law's case, there was a solid knock on my apartment door, and on the other side stood Raymond Dawson.

~*~

"Ray, wow. What a surprise," I said, totally caught off-guard. It had been more than a year since I had seen him, but I stepped back to open the door wider. "Come on in. It's good to see you."

Raymond was resplendent as ever. His wardrobe: African. Cream-colored slacks with gold tuxedo stripes down the legs, and a green, yellow, and gold dashiki that continued to just below the pockets of his pants. In walking, his movements were as smooth and purposeful as a dancer on stage, yet at the same time almost regal and mindful of the image being projected.

I closed the door and watched him from behind as he surveyed the room in much the same way as I surveyed him when he entered.

"You look good. How ya doin'?" I asked. "Where you headed?"

He didn't turn around when he responded as he walked toward the far side of the room to view a couple of prints hung on the wall. "I'm good," Ray said.

He stopped in front of a limited edition print titled, "Pussy Willow." It was a drawing of a young Black woman with a head of natural hair and who was holding a bouquet of pussy willows. It was the work of a talented local artist named Ellen Powell Tiberino, whose often thematically dark work Clara had introduced me to. I had a couple of her prints. I couldn't afford any of the originals.

"I love this picture," he said. "Where'd you get it?"

"A gallery up in Germantown."

Raymond finally turned around and said with a slight smugness, "I have the original."

I decided to let that comment slide. "You want something to drink, Ray?"

"What you got?

"Hard or soft?" I asked.

"Hard."

"Crown Royal."

"I'll have a small glass. With ice."

I headed for the kitchen while Ray stayed in the living room.

"Where you been this evening? You're all decked out but it's not that late," I said.

"Out."

"Oh? Just out? Dressed like that?"

"Afro-American history museum downtown. Another gala to celebrate the new Wilson Goode administration. Pointless, really," he said, finally walking into the kitchen just as I finished filling his glass with ice and pouring the drink.

I poured me one, too. Neat.

"He's the city's first Black mayor and all, but he's been in office for weeks. Things ought to be settling down by now," Ray said, though he added with a sigh, "But everyone was going to be there. To be seen. I dropped in for a second to make an appearance."

Looking good and making an appearance was something Ray started perfecting in our teens. Once in the summer after high school graduation and when I still attended church occasionally, I wanted to impress a girl named Lanese and needed a ride to the Sunday morning service at her church. I asked Ray for a ride and when I got to his father's place, I waited impatiently as Ray watched himself dance in front of a full-length mirror before getting ready to drive me. He dressed himself from head to toe in a white tennis outfit as if he was about to take Centre Court at Wimbledon.

He always operated on RST — Raymond Standard Time — which meant he got me to church late, though before the sermon started.

I never dated the beautiful Lanese and in all the years of our acquaintance, I've never known Raymond to play tennis. Not once.

Appearances meant a lot.

"Cheers," we said, clinking glasses and then walking back to the living room. I took the couch and Ray took a chair across from me.

"You know Allison Charles, the city urban development director?" I asked.

"Yeah. Not personally, really. But everybody knows her," he said, pausing as he looked directly at me. He had a devilish smile. "You gotta thing for her?"

Why do people keep asking me that? "No. Just asking," I replied forcefully, though that may have re-enforced his reason for asking. I then more quietly asked, "Was she at the event tonight?"

"I didn't see her," he said slowly, drawing out the words as he considered my question. "It was crowded, so she could have been, but I just didn't run into her. Why you askin'?"

"Just curious," I said, wishing I hadn't brought up the subject. I hoped he'd let it drop.

We were quiet for several awkward seconds as we both considered what to say next.

"You still doing your investigator-thing, huh?" he said finally.

"Yeah," I said, drawing out the word, knowing he was going somewhere with the question but hadn't yet finished the ride.

Ray sipped more of his drink and sat the glass down on a table to his right. "I think the head of security where I work is leaving in a couple of months. Retirement, I guess. It's about time. The position'll be open. If you're interested, I could put in a good word for you. I have some pull in the company, you know," he said, glancing around quickly. "And it might be a nice promotion for you."

From years of experience as a private investigator, I've learned that there's a moment with many new or prospective clients when they reach a crisis point — behind which there is an uncomfortable truth — and they wrestle with the decision of what to do. To tell the whole truth (or some portion of the truth), or not to be truthful at all and hope for the best. It doesn't happen with everyone but when it does, it's usually in my small office or in some neutral territory. Never in my home.

And yet, here was Raymond Dawson in my apartment hemming and hawing, and wasting my time with comments on my artwork or with job offers for positions that may never exist.

As a concession to our long association, I was willing to give him a little more time to come to grips with his uncomfortable truth, whatever it was. But I was tired and such patience was not infinite. I sat back on the couch, crossed my legs, and briefly waited.

He said nothing at first and avoided direct eye contact. It's then that I jumped in.

"Is that why you've come to my apartment . . . unexpected and unannounced . . . to gauge my interest in some non-existent job?" I said pointedly.

The word 'unannounced' caught his attention and he eyed me carefully. It took a while for the moment of truth to arrive. I could almost hear the gears in his head working as he came to a decision, which he fortified by reaching for his glass and downing the dregs of his drink.

"I've been seeing this girl. Audrey. You don't know her, I don't think. But you could have met her at some point with me. I don't remember," he said fast. "It's been a couple of years now and she wanted . . . more of a commitment. You know how it is," Ray said.

I didn't say anything, so he forged ahead. "I gave her an engagement ring a couple of months ago, back at Christmastime."

"Congratulations," I said with a forced cheerfulness that he didn't seem to notice. He was still mentally dealing with his uncomfortable truth.

"She's pregnant," Raymond said with a forlorn look that made him appear more vulnerable than I had ever seen before. But I wasn't expecting what he said next. "I need you to investigate whether it's really my baby."

CHAPTER VIII

We were bathed in sunlight filtered through stained glass.

My strained relationship with Raymond apparently didn't extend to others in my family, especially female members. While my father liked him, admired his social activism, and that he helped pull me out of my shell, my mother and grandmother adored him. Raymond's father was a widower, so they mothered him in ways that he didn't get at home, inviting him to family gatherings and cooking him his favorite foods. When they knew he was coming over, the house often smelled of oatmeal cookies baked with chocolate chips, Raymond's absolute favorite.

My mother always batted away his innocent flirtations when he'd enter the kitchen and open the oven for a whiff as the cookies baked. But I always thought she secretly enjoyed the attention.

A lot of that changed after I entered the military.

My parents died close together. Dad had a heart attack within a year after I left for the Navy. I was stationed in Europe but got leave and returned home to attend the funeral. Raymond was a pallbearer.

My mother, heartbroken as she was, was so proud to have her military son home. I stood next to her in my dress uniform, holding her hand, trying to be brave and supportive, something she did for me all my life. My sister Valerie and two brothers held it together well. But for me it was a short trip. I shipped out the next day.

It was especially hard when, less than a year later, I got the call from my brother Allen to come home immediately.

It was not a call I expected. My mother, who had been in decline since dad's death — a fact that they shielded me from — wasn't doing well and wasn't expected to survive. With another hardship leave, I took the first plane home, rushing from Philly international to Pennsylvania Hospital as soon as I was on the ground. I hadn't slept for nearly 24 hours but stayed up with my mother in the hospital room, talking and holding her hand.

Valerie, her eyes full of tears and her head on my shoulder, stood next to me on one side of mom's bed, while my brothers were on the other side, when my mother closed her eyes for the final time and her soul slipped away.

Raymond was called upon again to help carry the casket. It was the only time I remember seeing him shed a tear.

My brother Allen, an ambitious college freshman at the time, took mom's death particularly hard. It was a turning point for him. The direction of his life changed afterwards. He escaped into drug abuse to mask his pain, and somehow blamed me for being away from it all.

We haven't been close since.

The memory of those times and the grief I felt is why I hate funerals. I'm not alone in that, of course. Most people hate them. That is, most people under the age of, let's say, sixty-five. Elderly people, like my grandmother, seem to thrive on them.

Grammy Taylor attends funerals on a regular basis and knows all the protocols for the viewing, the service itself and for the repast afterwards. She and her friends know the locations of all the Black funeral homes in the city and visit them to pay their respects to the dearly departed.

Doesn't seem to matter whether Grammy Taylor was close to the deceased or not. She knew them, knew of them, or knew someone who was close to them. That's all it takes. Rarely does she venture to the graveside, in part because she no longer drives, but she attends viewings and most funeral services. Then she waits for the family to return from the burial at the cemetery to attend the repast to pay her final respects — and to comment amongst her friends on the entirety of the affair.

She and her friends would discuss how the body looked, the quality of the casket — "They spent too much money on that ugly casket. You can just bury me in a pine box. Don't waste money on an expensive casket," she'd say — how good or poor the service was, or how poorly the widow dressed. It wasn't unusual for Grammy Taylor to say, "She wasn't a godly woman when her husband was alive. I wouldn't expect much now. It's a shame."

I never pointed out the irony of passing such judgments. She is, after all, my grandmother and doing so would be disrespectful.

But as soon as I mentioned to Grammy Taylor that I planned to attend the service for Henry Cummings, she instructed me on the finer points of attending a funeral. For me, it was work. I wanted to see who came and perhaps make some sense of his murder. But for Grammy Taylor, it was more than that. It was a social event, and she insisted I make a good impression in case someone she knew saw me.

She read in the newspaper that the service would be at Beulah Baptist Church at 19th and Caleb. However, Craig's Funeral Home on 10th and Columbia was handling the body. "I wouldn't let that man get his hands on me, dead or alive," my grandmother often said of the owner of Craig's.

After Raymond left my apartment last night, I did as my saintly grandmother instructed and laid out my clothes for the service — dark and respectable but not all black. After all, I didn't know the deceased.

I dressed in a Navy blue jacket, white shirt with a red paisley tie, and charcoal slacks, and then headed out. While I didn't classify myself as a mourner, I wanted to arrive at the church early, and discovered that despite what Cummings might have been in life, he was popular in death. More than forty-five minutes before the service and the small parking next to Beulah was already full. I ended up parking more than a block away and walking back.

Beulah Baptist was a large stone edifice probably built in the early part of the century, around the time Black people in large numbers moved to North Philly from an area just south of the Independence Hall. Instead of one center aisle, the church had two aisles leading straight down to the communion altar. The pulpit and choir stand were slightly elevated behind the altar to allow the congregation good visual access. A massive wooden cross hung on the back wall above the baptismal pool.

There was a balcony for the overflow of the main sanctuary.

I positioned myself out of the way, in a corner in the back. But about ten minutes before the family arrived, Randolph walked in, and surprisingly, was wearing a blue suit. He spotted me and ambled over.

"What are you doing here?" he asked as he moved us to a seat further up but still along a far wall, under a stained glass window of Christ on the cross. We were bathed in sunlight filtered through stained glass.

"Paying respects and checking to see who shows up. And you?" I asked.

"Same as you, though I've done business with his operation from time to time," Randolph said. "Plus, I'll write a story for the paper."

"Who'll run the business now?" I asked in a quiet whisper.

"Not his wife. And not his sons. They aren't into that, I'm told. They have respectable jobs, far away from their father's gambling empire. There are a couple of fellas jockeying to take over but they're young and aren't ready. They'd ruin it," he said. "But I can tell someone in the last few days has been holding everything together."

I wanted to ask who that might be but the service was starting. Everyone stood as the family filed in. It was a large gathering led by his widowed wife.

The service was long but I somehow managed not to fall asleep. There were greetings and condolences read, four of his favorite songs were sung, two separate Scriptures were read — Old and New Testament — and three separate ministers in attendance but not specially mentioned in the program were welcomed to speak. They all spoke of his kindness and support in the Black community. All of that occurred before the eulogy by Beulah's pastor, who declared what a good and loving Christian man the deceased was, though barely mentioning Cummings by name. And when he did, he looked down at his notes, as if to remind himself.

Randolph greeted some of the family and close family friends as they left the sanctuary and headed out. I lingered behind, only joining Randolph at the top of the steps of the church as the family got into the cars for the ride to Eden Cemetery, which is quite a haul from Center City up in suburban Delaware County.

However, it was a sunny and unseasonably warm day for late February, so the trek wouldn't be too tiring. Tiring or not, I wasn't making the trip.

"Do you know his wife?" I asked, looking down toward a middle-aged woman dressed in a black wool coat and black hat with a veil.

"We have met several times. She likes a club I frequent called the Black Diamond down near Tenth," he said, as he tipped his hat in her direction as she entered the first of two long, black limos provided by Craig's.

"Those are her sons getting in with her?" I said.

"Yeah. They're worthless if you ask me," Randolph said, not hiding his contempt.

"You see any of his mistresses?"

Randolph faced me with a quizzical expression. "You kidding me? You can't swing a dead cat around here without hitting one."

"That can't be one getting in that second family car, can it?" I asked as a tall, stylishly dressed middle-aged woman, also in black, got into the back of a stretch limo. Two men near her age got in with her.

"Obituary says Cummings is survived by a brother, and a sister and her husband. They're from out near Pittsburgh. I think that's them," he said.

"That was a beautiful service, man, wouldn't you say Randy?" said a skinny, nervous-looking man who came out of the church to stand beside us. "Quite a sendoff."

"It was good," Randolph said. "How you doin', Chuckie? How's business?"

"Same ole, same ole," said the man named Chuckie.

To me, Randolph said, "David Blaise, this is Chuckie Johnson. Works for Cummings at the shop. Runs errands. He's my bookie."

"Nice to meet you," I said, shaking his bony hand. "What's going to happen next?" I ventured to ask.

"No tellin'. You'll have to ask me in a week or two." Chuckie said.

"I might come up to the shop, or meet you to talk about it," I said.

"I'll be there mostly. You can get me there most days," Chuckie said, before adding, "See ya, Randy."

"Yeah. See ya when your troubles get like mine," Randolph said in return as Chuckie headed down the steps and up the street. "I'll head back to the office to write this up. Can you give me a lift?"

We walked down the steps and headed in the direction of my car.

"Chuckie was intimately involved in Cummings' operation. And he knows all Cummings' women. You might want to talk to him as a starting point in finding the killer."

"Thanks for the advice and the tip."

They were worth more than the cost of taking Randolph down to The Tribune.

CHAPTER IX

"They're looking for a motive and you're providing a doozy."

I didn't closely follow local government or politics, as Randolph pointed out, noting that I didn't know what the DRPA was. But there are some local news headlines that are difficult to avoid. The highbrow Philadelphia Inquirer said:

MOBSTER SHOT, LEFT DEAD IN GUTTER

The more blue-collar Philadelphia Daily News, which included a picture of the dead man on the front page, shouted:

ROSETTI SILENCED.

The picture showed the bloody body of a man in a plaid sports jacket and dark pants lying in the street next to the curb, his arms outstretched and legs in a weird angle. He had been shot numerous times in the chest and torso. But the most memorable part was that his executioners had stuffed is mouth full of cotton balls, as if shooting him six times wasn't enough to silence him.

Such was the Mafia war in Philadelphia, dating back four years to the assassination of Mafia boss Angelo Bruno, who, with the approval of the five New York families, controlled organized crime in Philadelphia and Atlantic City. That business was still up for grabs, with a war going on between factions supporting Benito "the Baker" Patrese and Michele "Mikie" DelMarco. Carmen Rosetti was only the latest victim.

The mob war was the talk of the city, including several days later when I arrived at my grandmother's house for Sunday dinner. Unlike last week, when Valerie and the kids were called away, she and her entire brood were in attendance.

"Not safe to go out on the street no more," said Grammy Taylor, apparently returning to a conversation that started just before I walked through the front door. Acknowledging my arrival, she said, "Close the door and come set the table."

I noticed the main section of the Sunday paper sitting on a table next to the chair where my grandmother usually sat watching TV most of the day when she wasn't cooking. Other parts of the paper were scattered about the living room. She liked things neat and orderly, so she'd straighten up the room before she headed upstairs to bed around eight-thirty.

"I wouldn't worry much, Grammy," I said. "Mobsters rarely kill someone outside the mob family. And besides, it was in South Philadelphia, and you never travel down there."

"Never!" she said. "Look what would happen to me."

I found it funny that a little old Black lady in her late seventies, who would never consider doing anything improper, let alone illegal, would think some Mafia hitman would come after her. Even if they did, I'm sure they'd rethink the hit once they met her.

Grammy Taylor was a thin little woman with gray hair that matched the silver dress she was wearing, not having changed since getting home from the four o'clock service at her church. Sunday evening dinner was a tradition in the house but even if it weren't, Grammy Taylor's cooking — and the aromas from the kitchen that filled the house — would have drawn us in like a Pied Piper.

Tonight, the house again smelled of fried chicken. My mouth watered.

Grammy Taylor wore her white ruffled apron over her dress as she brought in a plate of sliced tomatoes, cucumbers, and scallions to the dining room table. I went into the kitchen and brought out a platter of chicken drumsticks, wings, and breasts. Valerie, who was followed from the kitchen by her six-year-old twins, Cora and Cody, was handling potatoes and green beans.

Last, Stuart appeared carrying macaroni and cheese, and a bowl filled with freshly baked rolls. That Stuart was helping was a miracle of God.

I had tried to talk to Stuart in the office for several days but his secretary said he was out of town and couldn't be reached. Valerie, however, told me earlier that he was back and would be at the house for dinner. I didn't relish talking to him in Grammy Taylor's house but I was determined to find a time and a quiet place to have a discussion.

As we arranged the food on the table, Valerie continued the conversation about the mob.

"The way I see it. . . ."

"The way you see it?" I interrupted playfully. "Who made you an expert on Organized Crime? You're a bank manager."

She punched my shoulder and returned to her train of thought.

"The way I see it, guys in Organized Crime spend, I don't know, a quarter of their time protecting themselves from being killed or in planning to kill someone else. At least right now. That means there's less time spent organizing crime that directly affects us. Mob murders are catchy and scary and, oh, get us all worried and riled up. But the truth is, the streets are safer for the rest of us," Valerie said. "Looks bad. Sounds bad. Might even smell bad. And it is bad for business development in the city, wouldn't you say, Sweetheart?"

Stuart, who was staring into space, didn't seem to be listening.

"Stuart," Valerie said, raising her voice to get his attention. "Organized Crime is bad for business development, right?"

"Ah, yeah, sure," he stumbled to get the words out. "It's not good."

"But the streets are safer overall, I think," she finally concluded.

"They teach you that at Temple?" I asked. "You should ask for your tuition money back."

She laughed and punched my arm again.

Grammy Taylor's place was at the end of the table closest to the kitchen, with Valerie sitting between the kids on one side of the table and with me on the other side. "Let's all sit down and eat before it's completely cold. Stuart you sit down there," she said, pointing to the other end, the Sunday dinner equivalent of Hell.

My grandmother never liked Stuart.

If she only knew.

I said grace and each said a Bible verse before we piled our plates with food and then ate.

"Too bad your girlfriend couldn't make it tonight," Stuart said to me, making some point, as we started eating. I wasn't sure what the point was but I was sure I didn't like it.

Valerie didn't like it, either, apparently. She gave him a look that ended the subject.

There was no scintillating conversation, which was amazing for a Sunday night dinner, and in fact very little in the way of chit-chat. We mostly covered downtown banking and the latest achievements of the six-year-old twins. But, for once, it was fine hearing that one twin lost a tooth and the other was head of their class, and that there were no further digs about Clara not attending the Sunday dinner.

As the table was being cleared, Stuart's chore was to take the dinner linens to the basement to be added to the whites already in the washing machine. That provided me with the opportunity to get him alone without drawing too much attention.

I headed for the kitchen.

"There's more Coke downstairs. I'll go down to get some," I said, closing the basement doors behind me. The stairs were narrow and old, forcing me to use the wooden railing down to keep from falling. And I once again thought: *These are a hazard for Grammy Taylor. She could fall and break something and it might be days before we knew it. We've got to have them replaced.*

I would talk to my brothers and to Stuart about that, but not tonight.

Stuart dropped the linens in the washer and turned to go back up but I moved to block him at the steps.

"You avoiding me, Stuart?" In such close quarters, his cologne filled my nose. It was the same scent as in the bathroom at the house of the murder.

"Why would I do that? You're the one blocking the stairs like a child."

"You hired me to look into a murder in a house you own," I reminded him.

"Shee, lower your voice," he said, holding a finger to his lips. "You want them to hear?" He looked up the stairs and then took my arm to steer me further into the basement and away from the steps.

"Did you find out anything?" he said.

"Of course, I found out something."

"What?" he asked, sounding impatient, as if he had not considered that I might figure it out. Obviously, he had less faith in my investigative skills than he initially pretended.

"You, Stuart. I found out about you. You lied to me."

He backed up an inch, as if it would help keep things quieter. "How did I lie to you?"

"Oh, pleeze. Don't be stupid. You said you had been *to* the house, not that you had *stayed* in the house. And you didn't stay there alone," I said, this time looking around myself. "You were there with Allison Charles."

Shocked appeared on his face. "How do you know about her?"

"Not the point. You just didn't think I'd find out?"

"I don't know what I thought," he said sheepishly, looking away. "Are you going to tell Valerie?"

"She's not the one you should be concerned with at the moment. The police are a bigger problem."

"The police? Why the police?"

I stared at him in shock, then looked around as if finding some random space in the dreary basement could clear my thoughts. Whatever I had thought about him in the past — and a lot of it wasn't good — I've never thought Stuart was stupid.

Until now.

"A dead man was found in the bedroom of the house you own and in which you are having an affair," I said. "That speaks to a possible motive for you to kill him."

"Motive? What motive would I have?"

"Oh come on, Stuart. Surely you can see this. Ray Charles could see it and he's blind," I said, straining to understand why Stuart missed the point. I drove it home. "Jealous. Because you weren't the only person having sex with Allison Charles."

"Jealous?" said Stuart, who started walking in widening circles in the narrow basement.

"And did I mention that he was naked when he was killed?"

"Naked?"

"Yes, Stuart," I said.

A high-pitched voice suddenly called as if from heaven. "You boys okay down there?" Grammy said from the basement door upstairs in the kitchen.

"We're good," I called up. "Just wanted to have a little manly talk with Stu."

"Don't be too long. I already put peach cobbler on plates in the dining room for you two. Hurry up, now, before the ice cream melts."

"Be right up," I said. Once I heard the door close, I looked Stuart closely in the eyes. "We're not through with this. I can't hide evidence from the police. It's against the law. And sooner or later, they're going to come to you and ask some embarrassing questions. And you had better have some good answers. They're looking for a motive and you're providing a doozy."

"Listen, Davey. You gotta believe me. I didn't have anything to do with whatever happened to that guy in that house. You gotta solve this for me. And quickly. That's why I hired you. Valerie doesn't know anything, and I want to keep it that way."

"We'll see," I said and he headed for the stairs, but I grabbed his arm to stop him. "But in return, I may need your help on another case I just got. It's for, uh, someone I've known for a while."

"What's it about? Who is it?"

"I can't tell you that," I said, then hesitated before adding, "It may be illegal. It's definitely a bit unethical. So, it's right up your alley."

He smiled.

~*~

I called Clara at home before I left my grandmother's house. "I'm just leaving Grammy Taylor's and I'll be over in a few minutes."

"I'll be here," Clara said.

I held my grandmother's hand as we walked to the front door. In my other hand, I carried a bag with two pieces of chicken, some green beans, and a slice of cobbler — part of a dinner for another day. We embraced and I kissed both her cheeks.

"It's too bad Clara couldn't make it this week. But we'll see her next week," she said, sounding less certain than her words. She was a perceptive woman and undoubtedly had a better understanding of my relationship than I had. Her normally cheerful eyes turned serious. "And you straightened Stuart out downstairs?"

"Yes, I handled things."

"Good," she said quietly.

"I'm gone, Valerie. Talk to you later," I called back into the house over my grandmother's shoulder. To her, I said, "Good night, Grammy."

I drove to 26th Street and Girard Avenue and circled the block until I found a parking space on 25th, which was near Clara's place. I let myself in with a key.

Clara was sitting up in bed, reading a Vogue magazine when I arrived. Taking off her reading glasses, she put down the magazine when I entered the bedroom. I removed my sweater and tossed it into a chair in the corner. It was on my side of the room and reflected my tendency toward disorder. She hated that and often mentioned that I could keep my own place looking like a pig sty if I wanted, but she'd appreciate my being neater in her house.

"How was dinner with your dysfunctional family?"

I smiled. "They missed you."

"I'm sure they did," she said.

"Yes. And my grandmother in particular said she's looking forward to seeing you next Sunday."

"She'd be the only one," Clara said lightheartedly, sliding her legs over the top of the bed and dropping her feet onto the floor. She walked around the bed to the chair, picked up the sweater and folded it.

She had on silk pajamas with short pants. They were fuchsia, a color I didn't like but that she loved. I got the set for her at Christmas at the Lord & Taylor store in Bala Cynwyd on City Line Avenue.

I reached around her waist and pulled her close. The kiss was long, hard, and passionate. I wanted her. She reciprocated. My hand slid down her back and under the waistband of the pajama bottoms, and cupped her sexy, round butt.

Breaking off, she looked up at me and said in a low voice, "You're ready, huh? What's gotten into you?"

"I just wish you were there with me."

I started unbuttoning her top as I kissed her neck. Once it was open and had fallen to the floor, I moved down to her breasts. Moving her backwards until we got on the bed, I stopped kissing her briefly to gaze down at Clara.

Her body was heavenly, her skin, flawless. Her arms were well-defined from using weights at the gym, her stomach was smooth and flat, and her legs shapely. She had a soft, round butt that she constantly complained of as being too big, but which I loved for its shapeliness and, from the front or from behind, she looked gorgeous in everything she wore.

We made love with a passion as if it were for the first time, but with an unhurried-ness that comes from two lovers who know each other's needs and are willing to satisfy them.

CHAPTER X

"I'm here to talk about Henry Cummings' murder."

Monday is not my favorite day. Most of the time, at least. But today felt different. I awoke feeling physically rested, and mentally clear and alert. I was greeted with the smell of hot coffee. Clara started the coffee maker before getting into the shower and it was done by the time she finished. She wore a silk robe and was at the end of the bed as I opened my eyes. My white coffee mug with a large eye in black was on the nightstand beside me, along with the morning paper.

"Good morning, Mr. Blaise," she said, bringing her mug to her lips, gently blowing over the edge onto the liquid before taking a tentative sip. "How are you this morning?"

I sat up and took my mug. I love the smell of coffee — well, who doesn't? — and closed my eyes as I inhaled deeply, savoring the aroma, and then opened my eyes to stare down into the tan colored brew.

Clara made excellent coffee.

I opened the paper and flipped through, landing in the sports section. Clara had the Metro section, which included another mob story, including pictures taken on the street outside the funeral home in South Philadelphia where Rosetti's service was held.

"You know what amazes me?" she said. "Look at these two pictures here." She turned the pages to me, and I looked up from coverage of a Sixers game. "I just know it was one of these guys who killed Rosetti. And they show up at the wake. It's insane."

Going back to the Sixers game, I absently said, "But it's their way, I guess."

"Davey, are you listening to me?"

Looking up again, "Of course I am. You said you're amazed these guys showed up."

"And this guy here," she said, pointing her finger at a short, well-dressed guy in what was probably a light gray overcoat with a black collar. "That's Benito the Baker. He's the head of the mob. What's he doing there? Paying his respects? That's bullshit. He's the one who probably ordered the hit. When he kills someone, he probably bakes pieces of his victims into pastries at his bake shop."

Clara was on a roll and when that happens, it's best to just go with it. She got up and walked around, stopping briefly at her dresser to get something to put on. "What's Benito gonna say to his widow or his orphaned kids?" she said, looking back at me as she put on underwear. "'Sorry, kids, but I had to kill your daddy. It wasn't personal. Just business.' Makes me sick to think about it. What hypocrites."

"I don't get it either but it's their way," I said, resigning myself to the reality that I wouldn't get back to the sports page until later. "I read somewhere that virtually all societies on earth have a prohibition against murder. Murder is universally wrong. What is different, what varies from society to society is what constitutes murder, as opposed to what constitutes justification for taking a life." Holding out my hands, as if to say, "I don't know," I said instead, "From the mob's viewpoint, taking a life isn't necessarily murder. It's all in the definition."

Clara looked at me as if I were speaking a foreign language she couldn't comprehend — and she was tri-lingual. My only recourse was to talk about something else. "What's happening with you at work today?" I asked. "I have to interview someone this morning about a case and I need to look really nice. What do you suggest I wear?"

I hadn't given her details of what I was investigating and wanted to keep her off the scent, so I fudged, but not by much. I hoped to get in to see Allison Charles and knew I'd need to look sharp. And my best clothes were in Clara's closet.

Clara bought most of it, and she liked dressing me. It was a game to her, as if I were a living, life-sized Ken doll.

Rising from the end of the bed, she moved swiftly to the closet with double doors and threw open the door on the left side. Several jackets and suits hung on an upper rack next to a line of shirts — some solid blue, white or dark green, followed by several striped shirts. Pants folded on hangers were below.

"How dressed up do you need to be?"

"I want to look nice . . . a shirt and tie, certainly . . . but casual. Slacks and a jacket will do. A suit will probably look too . . . formal."

"Ah-huh," Clara said, picking tan slacks, a tan jacket with vertical strips of green and darker brown, and a Hunter Green dress shirt. A tie matched the shirt. "These should do nicely."

I tried on the clothes just to get a feel of the look. Standing in front of a floor mirror, we studied my reflection for every angle, to both our satisfaction.

I undressed, showered, and dressed again, while Clara was getting ready for work, managing to do her makeup in front of a steamy bathroom mirror. After a final good-bye kiss, we left the house together.

I was in a surprisingly chipper mood.

I drove to my office to make the call to the Tribune as soon after 9 a.m. as I could. The paper published on Tuesdays and thus Monday was a deadline day. Randolph would undoubtedly be in the office early. Surely, he wouldn't be drinking at nine.

"Randolph, I need a favor," I said once I reached him. "Well, two favors, really."

He sighed into the phone. "I'm on deadline. Can it wait?" He sounded impatient.

"Well, maybe. One will probably take a little doin' and can wait. The other is more urgent," I said, and waited. But not for long.

Another sigh of resignation on the phone. "Tell me what you need."

"There's a woman, a pregnant woman, and I need to know who's the daddy," I said, sounding stupid and regretting asking it.

There was a silence on the line much like the quiet at midnight in a cemetery.

"Is this your girl, Blaise?" he finally said. "Why don't you just ask her?"

"I know this sounds suspect but believe me, it's not for me personally. It's for a client," I said. "And I told him the same thing . . . just ask her. From what I have been able to ascertain, he has no logical reason to suspect it's not his baby. But for whatever reason, he doesn't feel confident to ask."

"What, then, are you asking me to do?" he said.

"Is there a way to find some medical records?"

There was another long pause.

"Not legally, I don't think,"

"Randolph, I know you have sources everywhere. And all I want is to give this guy some peace of mind."

I heard him heavily exhale, which I took as a good sign. Finally, he said, "I assume she has a doctor and you know who it is."

"She does and I do," I replied.

"Give me her name and her doctor's name and I'll see what I can do," he said. I gave him the information. "And Blaise, no promises on this."

"Thank you," I said sincerely.

"What's the second favor?"

"It won't take much. I just need you to make a call and set something up for me," I said.

"What is it?" he was beginning to sound impatient again.

"I want an appointment with Allison Charles. Today if possible."

"Her again. What is it with her? You gotta thing for her?"

"No, I do not," I said forcefully, leaving no doubt. "We discussed this last week. Remember? You said you knew someone who could get me on her calendar and say I was a reporter working on a story."

"I *am* busy, you know. I have stories to get done today." Then he waited briefly, before continuing, "But I like you. I'll make the call and get back to you . . . in about an hour. That other thing, that'll take a while. Don't know how long."

He hung up.

Centerton had a client when I left to get a newspaper down at the corner. Back in the office, I settled into the Daily News' story about the Sixers/Bulls game, which I didn't get to finish before leaving Clara's house. Philadelphia won with a brilliant performance by Dr. J — a triple double: thirty points, ten rebounds, and ten assists.

The phone rang at five minutes to ten. "Had to call in a favor to get you on Charles' schedule today. She'll see you at noon. I didn't talk to her. Just the secretary. All Charles will know is that a reporter will be there to interview her. It's in her office in City Hall. The fourth floor."

"Thanks, buddy. I owe you."

"Right, you do. But keep me out of this thing with Allison Charles. That is, unless there's a good news story to it. Now, let me get back to the story I'm workin' on," he said.

~*~

I had nearly two hours before my appointment and the drive to City Hall would only take fifteen minutes, and only slightly more if traffic was bad. Determined not to waste the time, I headed out, planning to make a stop first.

I have a gun, of course, though I rarely carry it. But as a law-abiding citizen and because I'm a private eye, I have a current permit to carry a concealed weapon, which was issued by the Philadelphia Police Department's Gun Permit Unit located at 10th and Spring Garden. It's not easy to access their records but by greasing the palm of a clerk, I got access to the records I needed.

And there it was. Allison Charles of Philadelphia County had a permit to carry a weapon, although not a concealed one. I also checked to see if Stuart had a permit, only to remember too late that he'd probably get a permit in Montgomery County, which is where he lives.

I was surprised to learn he had a permit in Philadelphia County, as well.

I didn't plan to mention to either that I was aware that they had permits to carry weapons of the size and caliber that killed Henry Cummings. I would leave that surprise until later, when I knew more about the whereabouts of those guns.

I left just in time to get to City Hall at noon.

~*~

The hallways in City Hall are wide and the marble floors are clean and polished. And, when wet, slippery. I was glad it wasn't raining outside. The echo of heels on the marble floors bounced off the walls in the long, straight corridors.

Several people, civilians and security officers, were milling about outside the doors to the Mayor's Office, but no one stopped or questioned me as I stepped inside and approached a desk.

"I'm David Blaise. I have an appointment with Allison Charles."

"Have a seat and I'll let her know you're here," said the woman at the desk. I walked over to the wall and sat in a green leather chair. It was a short wait until my target appeared.

"Mr. Blaise, I'm Allison Charles," she said, extending her hand, which I took. Another firm grip. "Nice to meet you. My office is back here. This way," she said, extending her arm in the direction of the inner offices and leading the way.

Allison was more casually dressed than the last time I saw her but that was probably because last week she knew she'd be in front of television cameras. Yet even now in her office, she was striking in camel gabardine slacks with pleats, a maroon cashmere V-neck sweater with a maroon and camel-colored scarf, and flats. All of it was well-tailored for her tall, slender frame. And I was sure most of it was designer wear.

Allison had a moderately sized office, which was fitting given her relative position in the administration. It looked out onto the City Hall courtyard instead of out onto the street. But the decorations on the walls left little doubt of her connections and ambitions. There were pictures of her and Mayor Goode, several of Democratic members of City Council, a couple with people I didn't recognize and lastly, on the wall to the right of her desk, was a picture of her in the White House shaking hands with President Jimmy Carter. It would take some finely calibrated instruments to establish which one of them — Allison or the president — wore the broader smile.

She shut the door after I entered the office and escorted me over to two chairs separated by a small round table.

"Do I know you? You look familiar. Did I see you at the news conference last week about the Penn's Landing development?" she asked, studying me. "Yes, I think you were there. You stood in the back. Didn't ask any questions."

Good eye, I thought. "I was really just there to observe."

"If you like that project, you'll really be excited about what we're planning in South Philly along Delaware Avenue. A theater complex with multiple screens, restaurants, a place for games for children. It's very exciting," she said. "And there'll be plenty of parking. For free."

I was about to interrupt her with the business at hand but she was too quick. "This administration is all about economic development. We must be. It's what is going to drive the city forward for the next two decades," she said, hunching forward as if to drive home the point. "And if we don't fuel the engine of development, this city is going to be left behind. It's happening all over. In the suburbs, other big cities on the Eastern seaboard. New York, Washington. Look at what's happening in Baltimore, along the harbor. It's a game-changer. I don't want to see Philadelphia left behind. And Mayor Goode absolutely doesn't want that."

She finally stopped to catch a breath. I shifted in the seat to get more comfortable. I wasn't sure how she was going to react, but I wanted to be ready for it.

"I'm not really here to talk about development."

A crease appeared across her forehead and she sat back in the chair. "Someone put you on my calendar this morning saying you wanted to talk about economic development."

"That's not it," I said. "Not at all."

"If not, I'm not sure I can help you." Her hands were on the arms of the chair to push herself up. "My job is about economic development. If what you are looking for is about something else, you'll have to check with someone else in the administration."

"I'm here to talk about Henry Cummings' murder."

"I beg your pardon," Allison said, appearing caught-off-guard. She stopped getting up but left her hands on the arms of the chair. She also looked toward the door of her office, checking to see it was still closed. "Who? I don't know a Henry Cummings."

"Shot to death last week. It was in a house in Queen Village."

Her eyes searched mine, seeking to learn what I might know. "I think I remember reading about it in the papers. He was a numbers runner, right? His murder was connected to that, I think, according to the papers," she said. More relaxed, she added, "But I wouldn't know anything about it. I should probably put you in touch with the police."

"But you know the house. It's on Catharine. Near South Street."

"I don't think I do, Mr. Blaise. You have the wrong person." This time, she did get up, smoothing out her slacks as she did so. "I'll show you out."

"You were at the house the next day . . . the day after the shooting. That was the day of the news conference here in City Hall and you went to the house later that afternoon. You had on the same clothes," I said, which stopped her. "I saw you there. In the house."

Looking down at me, she asked, "Who are you, Mr. Blaise?"

"I'm a private detective and I'm investigating what happened in that house. So, you might want to sit down."

CHAPTER XI

"I assume youz knowz who I am."

"I don't know what you think you know but I've never been in that house, wherever it is," Allison said, though she didn't move toward the door.

I visited her with the most serious expression I could muster, and I leaned into it for emphasis.

"The day of the news conference. It was late afternoon, around five. You went to the house on Catharine, probably came in through the back door because the police were sitting outside in the front. It's how I got in. You went up to the third floor, but you didn't see me. You searched the third-floor bedroom and took something," I said, stopping briefly before pressing ahead. "I want to know what it was you took."

The room fell so silent you could hear our hearts beating. She cocked her head to the side as she studied me. "What are you after, Mr. Blaise?"

I studied her in return. "I'm after the truth, ma'am."

"Then you should go to the police."

"Is that what you want me to do? Go to the police? Even if they dismiss my allegations, they'll and come to question you about them," I said. "Is that what you want? Because eventually they'll make the connection between you and the owner of the house, Stuart Thomas. Perhaps even learn about your affair. How will that go over here in City Hall and with all your plans for economic development?"

She was still tense, cautious, and ignored my question, so I continued on.

"Were you there the night Cummings was killed? Was Stuart Thomas in the house with you?"

"I don't have to answer any of that."

"You will if I go to the police," I said.

"And they'll question you, too," she said. "They'll want to know how you know these things. And once they're thinking about it, perhaps they'll decide you committed the murder and are trying to pin it on someone else. *Me.* I do have powerful friends here in City Hall and in the police department."

"I don't think they'll suspect me. I have an alibi for that night," I said, though I had never pondered the question but knew it wasn't true for the time of the murder. But at the moment, it didn't matter. "Besides, I have a lot less to lose than you do with the police. Do you want to risk that?"

"What do you want?" she said.

"Did you kill Henry Cummings?"

"No."

"Were you there the night he was killed?"

"No."

"Do you know anyone who might want him dead?"

This time, she didn't answer right away. She looked quickly across the room then back to me.

"Ah, no. I don't know . . . ah, anyone . . . who'd do that."

"You certain?"

"I said no," she suddenly snapped and got up. "I think we're done here." Allison was at the door quickly in several long strides. As she reached for the door handle, she turned and said, "Thank you for coming, Mr. Blaise."

I stopped her from opening the door. "Just so you know, I really was there. On the third floor when you got there. You went into the bedroom. I was hiding behind the door to the roof deck. That's when I saw you."

I reached into my pocket and got a business card, holding it out to her. She was reluctant to take it but apparently, despite the tension between us, didn't want to be rude. She looked at the name on the card before she opened the door.

"If you think of anything else, call me," I said. "Number's on the card. Thanks for the conversation. It's been enlightening."

I walked out without looking back, though I heard the office door close heavily. It was all so dramatic.

On the way down on the elevator with two old white-haired people, I rubbed my eyes shut as I thought. Maybe I erred in confronting both Stuart and Allison about their affair. But I thought getting things out into the open might shake loose the truth. I certainly hoped — for the sake of Valerie and the kids — that Stuart wasn't involved in anything illegal. But if he was, it would come out. And I wanted to know it first.

~*~

For reasons only known to the gods, the confrontation with Allison Charles made me hungry. And it didn't help that by the time I left her office, it was one o'clock. While I was ready to get as far away from City Hall as possible, I debated whether to get something from one of the many street food vendors near City Hall, or head back up toward North Philly and find something up there closer to my office.

In the end, I decided on the Reading Terminal Market, which is only a couple of blocks east, down Market Street. Leaving my car parked on a lot on 13th Street, I was willing to make the short walk, though I had to turn my coat collar up to protect against the weather. And it's in such cold conditions that I question why I generally go without a hat.

Thank heavens it wasn't snowing.

The Reading Terminal Market was established nearly a century ago and is one of the oldest and largest public markets in the United States. It offers locally sourced produce, fine meats, delicious poultry, fresh succulent seafood, cheeses to die for, exotic and ethnic groceries, and some of the best baked goods available anywhere in the country. In addition, even the most discriminating food aficionado can satisfy their taste buds in any of a wide selection of eateries.

My favorite deli in the city is in the Market and serves my favorite sandwich — a Corned Beef Special — though known in other parts of the country as a New York Reuben. The Special is corned beef piled high on rye bread, with a healthy smattering of Russian dressing, coleslaw, and a slice of Swiss cheese.

I never skip the kosher dill pickle on the side.

Edging my way through the heavy mid-day crowd in the Market, I reached Howard's Deli halfway down one of the main aisles. Howard Greenbaum and his family were institutions in the Market, having opened the deli decades ago soon after arriving in Philadelphia from the Old Country, which, in this case, was Asbury Park, New Jersey.

Though the restaurant was crowded, Howard, a short, seventy-something-year-old balding man who closely resembled everyone's favorite uncle, saw me enter and waved me over to a place near the edge of a long counter, one of the few empty seats in the place.

"Ah, one of my favorite customers," Howard said as he wiped the counter in front of me as I hopped onto a red, vinyl stool. I didn't take the comment literally. He said that to most people he recognized but whose names had slipped his mind. "What'll you have, Boss? A Special?" Not waiting for my answer, he turned to the back to yell to the kitchen, "Manny, another Special for my customer."

"You know me too well," I replied. "But make it to-go, if you don't mind."

"No problem, Boss," he said. "How's the family?"

I nodded to him that everyone was fine just as I pulled out my notebook to jot down the notes from my meeting with Allison Charles and wait for my food. I was intrigued by some of her answers and wanted to get them down on paper — and some of my impressions of her — while they were still fresh in my mind.

Howard went away to clear dishes from a table near the front, then wiped it down and its two chairs before ushering over a couple of Asian tourists. But when he was free, I waved him over.

"So, Howard, how's business?" I said, stuffing my notebook back into my jacket pocket.

"*Comme ci, comme ca,*" he said, shaking his right hand in a manner to indicate indifference. "The fall was good, and the Holidays. But this winter, not so good. We're living off the hump."

I looked around the full restaurant with amazement and but didn't comment on what appeared to be a contradiction. "I guess the crowd from City Hall helps you get by."

He grabbed a bunch of white paper napkins nearby and started absent-mindedly wrapping silverware as we talked. "It's so-so. It's like that when there's a new administration."

I put my elbows on the counter and leaned in in a thoughtful way. "You hear gossip, though, about what's going on."

Howard stopped wrapping to face me directly. "Of course," he said in surprise but without sounding offended. "I hear things."

I gauged how to proceed but knew it must be done cautiously. People in the service industries surrounding City Hall — the bars, restaurants, and strip clubs — made a healthy living on the barter of information. But in this case, I didn't want it to get back to the subject of my interest, who, at the moment, was probably sitting in her fourth-floor City Hall office trying to figure out who I was, what I knew, and how much trouble I could create.

Therefore, I would judge Howard's willingness to talk and proceed based on that.

"Do you know Allison Charles?"

"No, not in person. Haven't heard much, either, though I hear she has nice gams," Howard said, more as a casual observation than out of any genuine interest in seeing those legs. "Economic development, isn't it? Smart. Been around the area for a few years. Graduated from Wharton. Joined the Goode campaign in the election last year."

Despite his modesty, Howard knew more than he generally let on. At least, initially. He was a good source because he knew where most of the bodies were buried in City Hall and when to share what information he had.

"Does she come in?" I inquired.

"I haven't seen her. Didn't during the campaign, either," he said, sounding disappointed. "Must not like Jewish food."

I smiled at the statement. Everyone in Philadelphia loved a good Jewish deli.

"I doubt that's the case," I said. "You hear anything about her from your City Hall customers? Anything interesting?"

Before he had a chance to consider the question, the ding of a bell caught Howard's attention and he turned to see my sandwich on a plate on the shelf in front of the kitchen. With his back to me, he placed it on a counter and wrapped the sandwich as he spoke.

"She's nice to people face-to-face but some people on the fourth floor don't trust her," Howard said, turning back to me, reaching under the counter, and pulling out a brown paper bag with a handle. "That's probably professional jealousy, because of her access to top officials, like the mayor." He wiped his hands on a towel and placed my order on the counter in front of me.

"What are you hearing . . . ah . . . about her personal life?" I asked.

Finally, a sly smile.

"I hear she's seeing a rich guy. Very hush-hush. Very secret, very discreet."

"North Philadelphia?"

"Don't think so. I hear it's a white guy. Must have some connections."

"Huh," was all I said. Reaching into my pocket for my wallet, I handed him a twenty-dollar bill for a $5.95 sandwich.

As I gathered up my coat and turned to leave, he said, "Be careful you don't get any of that dressing on your pants. It's hard to get the grease stain out."

"No worries. I'm going to eat at my desk when I get back to my office."

By the time I reached my office, I was half-expecting to see a pink slip showing that Stuart had called with the urgent demand that I call back. But to my relief, he hadn't, which gave me a little time to enjoy my lunch. Perhaps Allison hadn't gotten to him in the secret way they must communicate. After all, it wouldn't do either of them any good for a real estate developer and the city's director of urban development to be seen cozying up together. The knives would be out for the both of them.

"Is the detective in?" I heard from out in the outer office. It was a strong, deep, unfriendly voice. I was just wiping my mouth and downing a drink after finishing the last of the sandwich.

"And who wants to know?" asked Centerton, who was up front in his office.

A softer, higher-pitched voice, though not any friendlier, replied, "Who I am is no concern of yours. I'm here for the private detective David Blaise. Is he in?" This was the voice of a man in charge; the sound of a man who got his way.

Or else.

I got up and walked to the front. "I'm David Blaise. How can I be of help?"

There were three men, each impeccably dressed. And while I didn't recognize the two tall, strong men behind him, I recognized the short man with the high-pitched voice in front. And I recognized his gray coat with the black collar. I had seen it only hours earlier in the morning paper.

They came forward as a single movement. My heart stopped and my life flashed before my eyes. But my legs wouldn't move. I stood there, frozen in place, despite the impending danger.

"Our interests appear to be the same, Private Detective David Blaise. So I wantta hire youz," said Benito "the Baker" Patrese.

I had read that Patrese was a narcissist, ruthless in pursuit of his criminal business aims, and cold-hearted and brutal in his killings. Though he was a good six or seven inches shorter than me, he seemed to grow taller the closer he got. And now, here he was, in a space that only generously could be described as my office, only feet away in a cashmere coat with two lieutenants to back him up.

What was I to say?

"Hummmm. I don't know what you need but I'm sure you can probably hire a better detective. I only have a small operation," I managed to get out without my dry throat closing up.

"We will see," he said, then over his shoulder, he added, "Sally." The man to his right took Patrese's coat off his shoulders and folded it carefully over his own massive arms. Patrese marched past me and into my office proper.

Once in my office, he looked around and commented on it by sucking air through his teeth. He signaled for Sally, who handed the coat to his mobster companion and dusted off a stack of boxes for Patrese to sit on. Wouldn't want that black suit with wide lapels to get dirty. It wasn't my style, but I did admire the stick pin collar of his white shirt and gray silk tie. He had on a simple white gold wedding band, and large, gaudy silver rings on both pinky fingers.

The office was too small for all three of them to stand comfortably, so Patrese and I faced each other, while the henchmen/body guards stood just outside the door looking in. They weren't dressed quite as nicely as their boss, but they were still impressive.

And intimidating.

"Now we talk business. I assume youz knowz who I am," Patrese said.

I looked at him and then up at his two henchmen. "Yes, sir, I know. You're Benito Patrese." *I didn't say, You're the city's Public Enemy Number One. And the same with the feds.*

"This is good. This is good. So now we talk business," he said. "It's come to my attention youz are workin' the Cummings investigation. I wantta hire youz to find his killer."

"But I already have a client in that case."

"It doesn't matter. I hire youz. Pay you more. Youz quote me the figure."

"It would be unethical for me to take your money when I'm being compensated by someone else for the same work," I weakly protested.

"Private Detective Blaise, I was born in a rural Italian village," he said, which I knew was a lie. He was born in New York City. "I comes to this country as a babe. It was a simple life and I'm a simple man. A simple baker."

"With no disrespect, Mr. Patrese, you don't dress like a simple man," I said.

A sly smile reflected something all the press reports missed — he had a sense of humor, if only a slight one. "I take no disrespect, which is fortunate for you. But I always get what I want."

Patrese snapped his fingers and Sally reached into his pants pocket and pulled out a wad of cash. Had to be thousands of dollars. Sally peeled off five, crisp, new, hundred-dollar bills and dropped them on the desk.

They landed on a file regarding a confidential banking program my sister Valerie gave me as part of Centerton's case. I left the cash on the desk, untouched, but picked up the file, opened a desk drawer, and placed it inside. It was not the sort of information I wanted just anyone to see.

Large sums of money were being diverted from Centerton's accounting firm and into a hidden account at the bank. I was following a trail.

I looked at Patrese's cash but still didn't touch it. "I will tell you what I will do," I said. "I will hold this cash in an escrow account. And if my other client doesn't pay me, I'll accept your payment. Otherwise, I will return it to you when the case is over."

Good thing Valerie had previously set up an escrow account for me.

"Youz got the money, Private Detective Blaise," he said. "What youz do with it is up to youz."

"What do you want? And let me make this perfectly clear: I will not do anything remotely illegal. And I report anything I discover in any criminal investigation directly to the police. Otherwise, I could get arrested for withholding information."

He smiled at me in the same way a cartoon shark is drawn just before it chomps down in something. "Iz want youz to do what you must. Report to the cops if you must. I just want the information first. My retainer there, on your desk, buys me that much."

"How did you even come to know about me . . . or that I was looking into this case?" I asked.

"The bakery business is cutthroat, as youz might imagine. It's my job to knowz whatz goin' on."

"Then why do you need me? You clearly have other sources for information. Good ones. Better ones."

"This is true," he said, nodding his tiny head as a gentle laugh escaped his lips. "But I'm impressed by youz."

"Really? Why?"

"Youz got into the Catharine street house without the cops outside noticing. That was good."

"How do you know that?" I asked, surprised.

"My guys. They watch the house. They watch the cops. They see youz go in through the back."

And I thought I was careful. His people are good watchers for me not to have noticed anything. Not even Allison Charles knew I was in the house, even when she was.

"And the woman? They saw her, too?"

"Of course. I don't approve of her. She's a whore," Patrese said, shaking his head in disgust. "She sleeps with Cummings in the house owned by her lover. What type of woman does this? Ah whore. And anyone involved with such a whore deserves to die."

He stopped, as if noticing he was getting off-track. Looking around, he seemed to refocus. "But I wantta know her involvement in this," he said.

"Mr. Patrese," said the other bodyguard, speaking for the first time. He leaned forward to show the mobster his gold watch. Patrese got up and Sally draped his coat over the mobster's shoulders again.

"I will hear from youz. Salvatore here," he said, indicating Sally, "will keep me apprised of your progress. Youz keep the money."

I decided not to argue the point. There was no use. But I would put it in an escrow account, like I said.

CHAPTER XII

"You fucking, dirty rat bastard."

I was shaking most of the time during my unexpected appointment with Benito the Baker, and hoped he didn't notice. But notice or not, I had survived talking to one of the most dangerous and deadly men in the city. So now I needed to get out of the office just to clear my head. Besides, I needed to deposit the cash in the escrow account.

By good fortune, Centerton said nothing as I left, and I headed back into Center City to see my sister.

Valerie was the manager of the main branch of PSFS, the oldest savings bank in America. That she had risen to that level of responsibility was a testament to her dogged personality. And I was both proud and grateful. Proud, because a Black woman in such an important position was rare, and grateful because, at times, it afforded me access to financial information I wouldn't normally have.

The Philadelphia Savings Fund Society was in one of the skyscrapers downtown, and its letters graced the top and could be seen from miles away. The bank's main branch occupied two stories, giving the appearance of being open and accessible yet solid and secure. There were teller windows and offices for managers on the first level and offices for more important bank executives on the second level, although the bank's top executive officers remained hidden in offices much higher up.

"You have time for a walk?" I said after I stuck my head in Valerie's office. She was getting off the phone but waved me in.

"You look nice today. Something special happening? That why Clara dressed you? I know she did. You couldn't do this," she said, waving her hand up and down in front of me to indicate my clothing, "without help."

"Ha, ha, ha. Very funny," I responded, but pressed on. "You got time for a walk?"

She crossed her arms over her chest and stared back at me. "Okay, Davey, what do you want?"

"Can't a guy just stop in when he's downtown to say hi to his little sister? Take her out for a coffee?"

"A 'guy,' yes, could innocently stop by his 'sister's' office and take her for coffee," she said. "But you are not that 'guy.' Whenever you show up or call in the middle of the day, you want something. So spill."

"Valerie. I just stopped by for a chat."

She looked back at me in silence. Finally, she moved some papers around on her incredibly neat desk and then stood up. "Might be good to get out of the office for a few," she said with resignation in her voice. "I've been stuck in here all day." Then more forcefully, she added, "But this had better be legit, Davey. And I mean it. Let's go."

She grabbed her coat from a stand near the door, and informed an assistant we were going out for coffee and would be back in twenty minutes.

We headed south on 12th Street toward Chestnut and then Walnut beyond that. The coffee shop she liked was on the corner. As we walked briskly in the cold, we talked about her kids, one of whom had developed an ear infection, and about lazy brothers.

"It's scary downtown now, don't you think?" I said.

"No more than normal. Why?"

"What with all the murders and mob violence going on," I said.

"I guess. But that doesn't directly affect me. Nothing ever happens downtown. It's all down in South Philly."

"You're the manager of a bank," I said as a car passed by so close it was nearly on the sidewalk. "Shouldn't you be worried about that . . . like a robbery or something?"

"We have good security. And the main branch hasn't been robbed in years. The getaway's too hard. They'd have to get the money out of the bank and onto the street into some of the heaviest traffic in all of Philadelphia. They'd hardly get far before the police would catch up," she said, stopping to turn me to face her, as we were at the corner. "You angling to get a job? Some security work at the bank? I'm not the person to talk to."

"No, it's not that," I said and started crossing the street toward the coffee shop. When we reached the shop, I opened the door for Valerie and we entered. "What'll you have? I'm paying."

"Davey, the big spender." She turned to address the man behind the counter, placing her coffee order.

"I'll have the same," I added, getting the money and paying for both. Then I got back to my reason for seeing her, although I didn't tell her that. "I was thinking about your personal security. Around the house," I said, trying to sound casual as I leaned against the counter to my right and put my left hand on my hip.

"We live in a good neighborhood. There haven't been any problems up there," she said. I straightened up and thanked the guy as he handed us the coffees. We went over to a tall table with stools in front of the window. We watched people walking by, mostly heading west toward Broad Street.

"You guys have a gun at home?"

She thought for a moment. "I think so. No, now that I think about it. We don't anymore. We had a .38 for a while. But I didn't see the need. And I told Stuart it wasn't safe to have around the house because of the kids, even if it's unloaded. It's not in the house anymore."

"What happened to it?"

"Oh, I don't know. I think Stuart took it to his office but I'm not sure."

"You haven't seen it?"

"No. Should I have?" Valerie asked.

"I guess not," I said, though I wasn't sure I meant it. "Hope he doesn't carry it on him."

"I doubt it. He's a real estate developer. How dangerous of a job is that?" she said with a brief laugh before taking a sip of coffee.

"Might have to pistol whip some shady politicians to get some plans approved," I said, and we both chuckled.

We changed subjects and nattered on mindlessly for a while as we drank. When our cups were drained of coffee and only a grayish blob of undissolved sugar lay at the bottom of my cup, we left the coffee shop and headed back toward her office. The traffic light changed and we started across the street as I returned Valerie to the subject of her husband and guns.

"I think Stuart encounters difficult politicians all the time," she said, leading the way across the street.

"Yeah, that's got to be true here and in Harrisburg," I said.

"Like, he was in Harrisburg for a lot of last week . . . schmoozing and wining and dining lawmakers. But I think booze and butter-laden foods are what he uses to soften up people. Not the butt of a gun."

Harrisburg for several days last week, huh? But I saw him in his office during the day, on the day after Cummings was killed. Wasn't in Harrisburg then.

"Why all the questions? Is something wrong?" she said as we approached her building.

"Everything's fine. I'm just worried about your personal safety. I am a detective, remember?"

"Well, stop. You're worrying me."

We were at the revolving front door to the bank but hadn't

entered. "Valerie, I may need some help with something later. It's for a case I'm working."

"See, I knew it," she said, punching my chest with her pointer finger, a smirk appearing on her face. "I knew there was a reason you suddenly showed up and bought me coffee. What do you need?"

"A little later, after I figure a few things out."

Valerie gave me a good-bye hug. "Okay. Just let me know and I'll do what I can." She turned and headed into the revolving door. Looking back over her shoulder as she started through, she said, "And bring Clara next Sunday. No excuses."

No excuses, indeed.

~*~

Centerton left the office early, leaving me alone after I got back from coffee with Valerie. I was glad for the solitude. Afforded me some time to think without distractions. I was coming to the end of his case but wasn't ready to report my findings.

Frankly, I preferred to see or talk to Centerton as little as possible. I never had such trouble with his partner, Leslie King. But I suspected, at the end of my case, that would dramatically change.

I was tempted to call Raymond with an update on his case, but still I had little to report. I wondered why he was so adamant about finding out if he was the father of his unborn child since at this point it would be difficult to conclusively determine. And he hadn't given me any indication that she was seeing anyone but him. There must be something he wasn't telling me. I was pondering that and packing up when the phone rang.

Damn.

"David Blaise Investigations."

"You fucking, dirty rat bastard."

I knew I shouldn't have picked up the phone. It was after five by then and it had been a long, busy day. I should be gone. But I decided to take just one last call. Too bad there was no way to determine who was calling before picking up the telephone.

What a fool. Because, finally, it was Stuart. I had nearly forgotten about him.

"You rotten son-of-a-bitch. You had to go and talk to her, didn't you? Had to stick your skinny ass in my business," he said.

I could almost see him frothing at the mouth. And I wanted to remind Stuart that I had him by the balls and could destroy his personal life and vastly complicate his professional life at any moment. Therefore, swearing at me wasn't a good idea.

However, I didn't say that. I went with what I knew was his greater problem.

"Stuart, you asked me to look into Cummings' death, did you not? Did you think I wouldn't find out about Allison? For goodness sake, man, give me some credit. It's why you hired me in the first place."

"A regrettable decision made in a moment of weakness," he said, though he had calmed down a little.

"That may be so, Stuart, but you have problems. I mentioned as much to you last night. Remember?" I said. "By the way, I've never asked you this and should have. Where were you on the night Henry Cummings was killed?"

"Home, with Valerie, I think, and the kids."

"You think? You're not sure?" I said, wanting to shout into the phone. "You must know, Stuart. Sooner or later the police are going to come and ask. You need to tell them the truth, because they'll check."

"I was home."

Not in Harrisburg, I wanted to say. "Okay then," I said, accepting the lie. "Allison must have called you this afternoon."

"Yeah, said some two-bit, asshole detective came by the office this afternoon . . . muscled his way in, actually, saying he was a newspaper reporter . . . and was trying to pin something on us."

"What did you say?"

"I acted surprised. I couldn't very well say, 'That's just my asshole brother-in-law.'"

"She remembered my name?"

"Allison remembers everything."

That I could believe. She remembered me from just seeing me in the background of a press conference days earlier, even though I never said a word that day, let alone spoke to her.

"You're not going to mention any of this to Valerie," he said, sounding both worried and desperate. "That's our business arrangement."

"She may very well find out, Stuart. You're cheating on her and women have a way of finding out such things. Don't ask me how. They must have some sort of radar that says their husbands are having too much sex," I said. "But our arrangement is intact. She won't hear it from me, though she very well may hear about it. But it won't be from me."

I heard him sigh on the other end of the telephone and could almost see his body begin to relax. "Okay, but it can't be from you," he said.

"No. When she does find out, it should be from you, not someone else, like someone from the police," I said. "This case is getting very interesting, although I'm no closer to solving it. Let me think and I'll call you tomorrow morning. Where will you be?"

"At the office by eight-thirty," he said.

"I'll call sometime after that."

I hung up the phone, finished the rest of what I was doing and headed out, locking the door behind me, insuring that I wouldn't answer the telephone again if it rang.

I hadn't talked to Clara today and couldn't do it now. I was tired and all I wanted to do was sit on the couch, eat some fast food, and rest before going to bed.

I couldn't find a parking spot near the apartment and had to walk back more than a block-and-a-half. If it wasn't for the necessity of getting around freely, I'd get rid of the car. In addition to the hassle of finding a place to park — especially near the Penn campus, where getting a spot is always tricky — the cost of insuring the car and regular maintenance were financially crushing. Mrs. Findley had neither a parking space nor a garage for me. My only option was hoping to find a space on the street nearby.

As I entered, I noted that Mrs. Findley was baking something, perhaps cookies or a cake, judging from the aroma filling the hallway of the building. I continued up the stairs toward the second floor.

"Oh, God, yes, yes," I heard a female voice say through the thin walls of the second floor across the hallway from me.

I guess the college roommates are home, I thought. I was tempted to bang on their door but decided against it. They had so much loud sex I wondered when they ever had time to study.

Inside my apartment, I dropped the keys in a bowl beside the door, turned on the television and plopped down on the couch. Except for the glow from the TV screen, I left the room dark, intending to sit for a moment to catch a little shut-eye before changing into more comfortable clothes and eating dinner. But exhaustion dragged me into a deep, dreamless sleep. When I woke up, the 11 o'clock news was on and my shirt was soaked in my sweat.

After turning off the television and making sure the apartment door was locked and chained, I managed to drag myself to the bedroom to undress and quickly climbed into bed. Eating would wait until morning.

CHAPTER XIII

"I'm Michele DelMarco but my friends call me Mikie. I'd like you to call me Mikie."

I was up early because I went to bed so early, if you include the time on the couch. I thought I talked to Clara before I went to sleep but I wasn't sure.

I had been too busy in the last week to get in my regular exercise regimen — an early morning run along the Schuylkill River on East River Drive. So with no pressing business early, I decided to get in a run. I changed into several layers of sweats and went to the car. It promised to be a good run because it wasn't a particularly cold day for February. It was the mildest it had been in several weeks. Clear and crisp.

I drove to the Art Museum and parked in back. After a stretch, I started my run on the walking/running path, which coursed parallel to the road. I headed a quarter-mile to Boathouse Row, and gathered steam as I ran up toward the Falls River Bridge. Inbound traffic headed for Center City whipped past at breakneck speed in the opposite direction. At the Grandstand Curve, the fence separating the running path from the traffic was so short and so weak, I was sure some car would come barreling through and kill me one day. But it hadn't happened yet, thank the Lord.

I sweated through every layer of my clothes by the time I returned to the car forty-five minutes later, and body heat fogged up the interior windows on the drive back to my apartment. The damp clothes felt cold on my skin and I looked forward to a nice, warm shower when I got home. The phone was ringing as I entered the apartment and, for some reason,

I decided to answer it instead of letting the machine take a message.

That was a regrettable decision.

"I need to see you right away, at the station," police Detective Thompson said immediately, not even waiting for me to say a word. There was a mixture of urgency and irritation in his voice.

"What's up?" I said, using a towel to once again wipe the sweat off my brow, forehead, and neck.

"We can talk when you get here. Be here in forty-five minutes."

I was about to say, "Forty-five minutes?" but he hung up too fast. Lots of people were doing that to me: making one last and final statement, and hanging up before I had a chance to respond.

I vowed to stop answering the phone.

Eating took no time, and a hot shower took even less. But both felt good. I dressed in jeans, a white shirt and a sweater and headed out the door in a light winter jacket.

I failed to notice him at first as I walked down the front steps, but a man in a heavy, brown overcoat was leaning against a brand new Buick four-door, which was doubled parked, forcing eastbound traffic to go around. As I reached the sidewalk, he stood up and said, in a no-nonsense voice, "David Blaise. Someone wants to speak to you." He opened the back door on the passenger side and added, "Get in."

I gauged the situation. If he wanted to shoot me, he would have already. But I didn't want to get into a stranger's car. I thought of turning around and heading back into the apartment building but he must have considered that, too.

"Don't make me come after you," he said.

I doubt he could have caught me even if he wasn't wearing an overcoat. But shooting me might be an option. The seriousness of his tone showed it was an option he'd take.

From inside the car, a polite voice said, "Please, Mr. Detective. I just want a minute of your time."

I could see a single individual in the car and made two decisions on the spot. I'd get in the Buick, and if I survived, I'd start carrying my gun. Concealed, of course.

Once I was inside the car, the guy outside closed the door. I expected him to come around and get in the driver's seat but he just stood outside, his hands clasped in front. It was comfortably warm inside, like they had been waiting a while, and the seats were a plush leather.

All mob figures must get their suits tailor-made in some specialty shop in the Garment District. His manicured hand extended beyond a shirt with French cuffs held in place by gold cufflinks. He introduced himself.

"I'm Michele DelMarco but my friends call me Mikie. I'd like you to call me Mikie," he said. He stuck out his hand and I considered it would be the height of disrespect, given the circumstances, not to accept it. His hands were soft, as if unaccustomed to doing hard, physical labor, but his grip was strong and firm, an indication of his willingness to command hard work by others.

"My friends call me David."

"David. I like that. It's Biblical," he said, sounding very pleased with himself.

"I generally don't think of it in that way but yes, it is."

"David. I like it," he said, glancing up at the ceiling in the car, as if he was going into deep thought. His tone was friendly, conversational, without the slightest hint of a threat, even when he immediately changed from the subject of our names. "I want to discuss something very personal to me, David."

I had read articles about DelMarco. Though coming from a mob family, he was cultured and well-bred, having gone to an elite private school in New Jersey. He shunned publicity but when he did seek it, it was always in some philanthropic endeavor, such as a Christmas party for poor children in South Philadelphia or South Jersey. He was always donating something for some cause. It provided a degree of goodwill — to mitigate his violent, criminal behavior.

But in my take of the on-going Mafia war, DelMarco didn't have the upper hand. And it was only his innate understanding of people and their motives that kept him alive.

"I have learned that you had a meeting yesterday afternoon in your office on North Broad Street with . . . one of my business competitors, you might say. Benito Patrese," he said in a voice that spoke of breeding and a cultured education. His diction was impeccable. Every consonant was as clear and crisp as the weather outside the car.

"Competitors? That's putting it mildly," I said, with more confidence than I should have any reason to have.

"Competitor, yes," he said with a smirk, much like that of a lion just before biting off the head of his prey.

"He stopped by my office unexpectedly. And, frankly, the meeting was unwelcome," I said.

"That's very much like him, to impose himself unexpectedly on people," DelMarco said.

Just like you're doing to me now, an ironic point I wanted to make, but I held my tongue.

He continued. "David, as a new friend, I would very much like to know the substance of your conversation with my business competitor."

I swallowed twice to give myself a second to consider my answer. He waited patiently. "He wanted to know about a case I'm working on."

"The killing of Henry Cummings. Yes, I know. Very unfortunate. So much violence in the city these days. And danger," he said, sounding sincere. "And you told him what?"

"Nothing, really. I haven't learned very much. Besides, I couldn't disclose it to him even if I had learned anything. I'd be divulging privileged information of my client's, which I can't do."

"That's a very honorable thing. I appreciate that, a sense of honor. So much of it has been lost these days," he said, shaking his head. He curled his fingers toward his face and casually examined his manicured nails before speaking to me again. He didn't look up. "But David, there is a difference between keeping privileged information secret and keeping a secret for no reasonable purpose." Then he looked at me. "I trust you know the difference."

I don't think I perspired this much during my morning jog. "I believe I get your meaning."

"Good," he said, pressing a button and rolling down my window. "I'm ready," he said in a louder voice through the window. The door was immediately opened. To me, he said, "I'm glad I have a new friend and we've had such a wonderful meeting of the minds. I'll be in touch."

I got out of the car and it quickly drove off. My knees were so shaky it's a wonder I managed to remain standing. However, fortunately, I had only a short walk to my car. Despite feeling less than prepared for whatever he wanted, I didn't want to be late for my encounter with Detective Thompson.

I was calmer and in better control by the time I reached the police station, and was ushered in. Thompson didn't stand as I approached, "You're late," he said angrily. "I said forty-five minutes." Before I had a chance to respond, he indicated the chair next to his desk. "Sit down," he demanded.

"I thought I made myself clear last week about not getting in the way of our investigation. But you obviously have decided to ignore my advice," he started angrily.

"I've had a stressful morning but let me assure you, I have no idea what you're talking about."

"Oh, really?" he said. His hand went into a desk drawer and retrieved a manila envelope. Reaching inside it, he pulled out several black and white photographs. "And you don't know any of these guys?"

He spread the pictures out on his desk for me. They were of excellent quality and the faces were easily recognizable. The photographer, who took the shots from a distance with a wide-angle lens, knew what he or she was doing.

"That there is your office. And these three gentlemen have just come out of your office. Let me identify them for you in case their names have slipped your memory." He tapped one photograph as he spoke. "That's Benito Patrese in front, getting in the car. Big Salvatore Ricci is the one holding the car door open for Patrese and that's Joseph "Little Joey" Bianchi walking around to the driver side to get in the car. Ricci and Bianchi are underbosses in the Patrese organization. And they all came to visit you."

Thompson stopped and gave me a long, serious stare. It was hard for me to return the look but I didn't back down. It was a matter of professional honor not to be intimidated.

"What do you want to know, Detective?" I asked.

"Why did the head of the Philly mob come to visit you?" he said, also not backing down. "And what are we to make of that?"

"You been watching me, Detective," I said, adding, "I'm flattered."

"Don't be smug, Blaise, and don't flatter yourself," Thompson said with a certain smugness of his own. "With all the mob hits, we keep an eye on these guys. We didn't have reason to keep an eye on you. Until now."

I picked up a picture, examined it and returned it to the desk.

"Yes, Patrese and his boys came to my office. You know that. But I didn't invite them. I'd never met any of them before. I was completely surprised when they showed up."

"You expect me to believe that three top mobsters just suddenly showed up at your doorstep?"

"That's what happened. Patrese asked me about the Cummings murder and I told him what I told you. I don't know anything," I said, stopping to consider my next statement. "It's also what I told Michele DelMarco when he dropped by . . . also quite unexpectedly, by the way . . . at my apartment this morning, right as I was headed over here. He asked me to call him Mikie."

"You met with DelMarco?" He suddenly looked concerned.

"Obviously. That's what I just said. It is good to know you aren't watching me all the time." I waited for a response and when Thompson said nothing, I continued. "I was leaving the house and found him waiting outside for me in his car. It's why I was late getting here. He wanted to talk. Seems a lot of people are enormously interested in the Cummings case. I wonder why?"

Thompson gave me a long stare. "I told you to stay out of the way, Blaise. You think this is a game? Well, it isn't. It's serious business. I intend to get these guys and send them all to jail where they belong."

"Whether I think it's a game or not isn't relevant anymore. You know what is relevant?" I said. "It's you asking me questions, mobsters dropping by uninvited and asking questions, other people asking questions. I guess I'm in this thing whether I want to be or not. That's what's relevant. And there's one more thing."

"And what's that?" Thompson said.

"There's got to be a leak in the police department," I said, seemingly shocking Thompson in the process. He shouldn't have been but law enforcement officers are quite sensitive about police corruption.

"Given the size of the department . . . How many officers do you have? Seven thousand or somewhere in that ballpark . . . neither one of us is surprised. Or should be," I said.

Thompson scratched the back of his head and leaned back in his chair to consider my statement. "What are you saying?"

"I assume this is super-secret. And yet, someone knew about this meeting to get these photos quickly to you," I said. "Think about it. It's a possibility and you should be looking into that."

Thompson hurriedly collected the photographs and stuffed them back in the envelope that went back into his drawer. He slammed it shut.

"Go on and get out of here, Blaise. And don't leave town. We aren't through with you yet."

I got up to leave. "It's the furthest thing from my mind."

The closest thing on my mind wasn't that clear to me.

CHAPTER XIV

Even from a distance, there was something familiar about the dead man.

Just as I was leaving, Thompson got a call. After speaking for a moment, he looked up at me and then slammed the phone down.

"You're in over your head, Blaise. But you need to go," he said hurriedly. Then Thompson raised his voice so everybody in the room could hear him, "There's been another Mafia hit. Just got the call. Officers are headed to the scene. Where's O'Donnell? We gotta go."

Several people scurried around, grabbing their gear and adjusting the holsters for their weapons. Thompson's young partner came running in, stopping at the desk. He spoke first.

"I just heard. Do we know who?" he said.

"No, call just got here. But it's in South Philly. On a corner," Thompson said. "Let's go."

"I'm coming too," I said.

Thompson turned back and pointed a finger at me when he spoke but he kept walking away. "You stay out of this, Blaise."

The hell I will, I thought. And I followed them out.

~*~

At three centuries old, Philadelphia is an old city, though compared to Boston it's still a youngster. And like most large Eastern cities, its oldest streets tend to be narrow. But unlike Boston, the oldest part of Philadelphia, running from the Delaware River westward, was planned, at least in its initial stages, by founder William Penn. Its narrow streets are on a grid but tend to be straight, whereas Boston's oldest streets tend to meander.

A Philly exception is Passyunk Avenue, which cuts through the city like a knife, slicing at an angle through South Philly. It's hard to find parking on Passyunk because of all the good local eateries and shops along its path. And it was outside one of those eateries, and less than two blocks north of one of the city's most famed cheesesteak restaurants, where the latest mob hit occurred.

I found a place to park three blocks away, and followed the flashing lights atop police cars and the tall antennas of TV trucks to the scene. We were kept at a distance but I could see a body on the ground outside a candy store. Blood was everywhere, on the side of the building and on the ground where he fell. It was gruesome, and yet still drew a large crowd.

The area was overrun with police, some standing over or near the body, while others interviewed witnesses and conducted crowd control. But even from a distance there was something familiar about the dead man.

I spotted Randolph, who was taking notes and directing a Tribune photographer about where to get a good picture. I made my way through the crowd to get to his side.

"Hey, Randolph. You heard."

Surprise played across his chiseled face when he saw me. "Blaise, what are you doing here?"

"I was having a chat with police when the call came in. I followed them over," I said. "Who's the victim? You know?"

"Haven't gotten word from the police yet," he said.

By then, I had my best view of the body and I instantly recognized the victim. "It's Little Joey Bianchi. He worked for Patrese," I said.

"You sure?" Randolph asked as he wrote down what I told him but also looked up at me as if to say, "How do you know that?" I answered the question before he asked it. "I recognized him from a picture I saw when I was talking to the police."

"Excuse me," he said, closing his reporter's notebook. "That's the press gal from the Police Department." I followed where he was looking and saw a woman in a police officer's cap and wearing a blue uniform with markings on her shoulders. "I need to talk to her," he said, heading off. Then he stopped briefly to get my attention again. "But when I get back, I have some information about the pregnant lady friend you asked me about."

I stayed put, somewhat transfixed with horror and fascination. Detective Thompson caught my eye. He stopped talking to a uniformed officer and walked over to me.

"See," he said, flipping his thumb over his shoulder in the direction of the dead man, "These guys are serious, David." It was the first time he had addressed me by my first name. We had just crossed a barrier of trust that, until that moment, I didn't know existed. "You need to be careful."

"Do you think this has any bearing on the Cummings case?" I asked.

"I can't see how it would, but I don't know," Thompson said, rubbing his hands together and blowing on them to warm them up. Through his cupped hands, he added, "We'll have to see."

"I'll keep that in mind, Detective. And I think I recognize the shooting victim there," I said, indicating the dead body still lying on the sidewalk.

Thompson's knitted his brows, and glanced back and forth between me to the body. "Oh? Who?"

"Joey Bianchi. One of Patrese's boys. He was the driver of Patrese's car," I said. "Check the pictures you have from yesterday. You'll see it's him. And so maybe this *could* be related to Cummings' death."

"Blaise, that could be just a coincidence. There was already a mob war going on before Cummings was killed," Thompson said, absentmindedly scratching his head, which I noted he did when he was deep in thought.

There was no more for me to do, so I took my leave. "You'll excuse me, won't you?" I said. Thompson gave me a wordless nod as he walked off.

Randolph was finishing up and talking to his photographer when I wandered over.

"I think we're done here for the moment," said the photographer, a tall young man with a head full of dark black dreadlocks. "Not much more I can get here. I'm headed back. You comin'?

"N'all," Randolph said to his colleague. "You head on back in. I'll be there in a while and look at some of the pictures when I get there."

As the photographer left, Randolph took a firm hold of my upper arm and pulled me to the side of a building.

"The police haven't confirmed the identity of the dead man but, when I mentioned it to the press aide, she didn't deny it, either," Randolph said. "Thanks for the tip." He then lowered his voice to a hushed whisper. "I had to call in some serious favors to get anything on that other matter you asked about."

"I understand," I said, nodding in agreement. "What have you got?"

"The pregnant woman's doctor, Norah Paine-Simpkins, has her main family practice office up in Mt. Airy, but is also part of a midwife practice for delivering babies over at Hahnemann University Hospital," Randolph said.

"How pregnant is she?" I asked, though I knew instantly how stupid that sounded. You are pregnant or you're not. There are no degrees of pregnancy, only periods of gestation, which was really what I wanted to know. "Do you know how many months she's pregnant or when she's due?"

"Not specifically right now, but she's in her final months," Randolph said. "I can probably get a little more information, but it'll violate the patient's privacy so it's gonna cost you some cash."

I thought for a second about my last conversation with Raymond Dawson. There was something about it that was nagging me but I couldn't put my finger on it. "No, why don't you wait a little before we cross that bridge?"

~*~

The scene of this latest mob assassination was not far from the Catharine house, and I decided to play a hunch. There were no officers outside — they were all undoubtedly at the current murder scene — but I still went around the block, paying close attention for any prying eyes. I entered the house again from the patio in back but instead of going upstairs, I headed to the basement.

During my talk with Stuart in Grammy Taylor's basement, he said there were places in the house to conceal important things. Didn't mean much at the time, but now. . . .

The basement was finished with wood-paneling walls and track lighting on the ceiling. It was mostly empty except for the furnace, water heater, a washer and dryer, and blowers for the heating and air conditioning. Since no one lived in the house, there wasn't much reason for people to come down there.

As I looked around at all the walls, they all looked the same. Except one.

It was the rear exterior wall. I went over and placed an ear to it. Nothing. Then I tapped it. Sounded solid. I tapped more places. More of the same. Finally, I tapped a spot and the sound was different.

Hollow.

There was a seam, which resembled all the other panel seams, but I pushed the panel and it opened, revealing a recessed area that contained a gun and more cash than I had ever seen in my life.

"Uh-huh. What have we got here?" I said aloud. Then I looked around, hoping that there wasn't a sound recording system in the basement. I saw no clues of one, and turned back to the recessed area. I examined it closely and didn't touch either the gun or the cash without a handkerchief in my hand. I wiped down the few things in the basement that I might have inadvertently handled.

I was determined to get out of the house without leaving a trace of my presence.

~*~

I had to talk to Stuart and didn't want to do it on the phone. I drove up to his building and was stopped at his office door by his secretary.

"He's very busy, sir, and can't be disturbed," she said at her desk, with his closed door behind her. Problem was, a long, vertical window with clear glass was next to the door. I could see in — he really was on the phone — and he could see me. So I just walked in on him, with his secretary right behind.

"Excuse me, Mr. Chairman," Stuart said into the phone as he stood from behind the desk. Holding the phone to his chest to muffle the sound, he said, "What are you doing in here?"

"I'm so sorry, sir," his secretary said in a rush of breathless nervousness. "I tried to stop him. Told him you were not available."

"We can talk now or I can talk to some friends downtown," I said.

Stuart exhaled heavily. "You can go, Susan. And close the door." He lifted the phone back to his face and said into the receiver, "I'm sorry, Mr. Chairman, but an emergency has just come up and I'll have to call you back later this afternoon once I handle this. Yes, yes. If I don't get you in your Harrisburg office, I'll call your house in Gettysburg in the evening."

He hung up the phone and sat back down in his chair, doing both somewhat harder than he should. "What is it that's so all-fired important that you barge into my office and interrupt a call to the chairman of the state Senate Appropriations Committee?"

"I truly don't think you grasp the potential gravity of this situation, Stuart. Getting to the bottom of this, and getting there truthfully, could spell the difference between the success of your business and family life . . . or its destruction. It's not something to play with," I said.

"Damnit, man, that's why I came to you."

I got up to stand over his desk. Placing both my palms flat on its surface, I leaned over it to make my point. "Then stop lying to me, Stuart. Tell me the truth."

"About what?"

I threw my hands into the air in exasperation and turned away from him. "Everything. First, where you were the night Cummings was killed," I said. I faced him again. "You told Valerie you were in Harrisburg most of the week but you called me to your office the next morning. And that's just the beginning."

He arranged some things on his desk and then leaned back in his chair. To further stall for time, he brushed off the front of his white shirt and straightened his tie. It was one I gave him for Christmas. (Actually, Clara bought it at Bonwit Teller on Chestnut Street and gave it to me already gift-wrapped. I saw it for the first time at a Christmas dinner when he unwrapped it.)

"I worked very late here in the office, ate here, and then had a drink with, well, you know who."

"Allison Charles."

"Yes. Allison."

"Where?"

"Her place up in Fairmount, off of Twenty-sixth Street," he said.

"Anyone see you there?"

"No. We were alone."

"Anyone see you leave?"

"Good Lord, I hope not."

I turned away from him. "You're an asshole. And I should just let your stupid ass rot." I turned back to address him directly. "And I would let your ass rot except that I don't want to put my sister . . . *your wife* . . . or my niece and nephew . . . *your children* . . . through hell. That's all that's saving you right now."

He dropped his head down, refusing to look me in the face. It was probably the nearest he could come to displaying contrition.

"Will she . . . Allison Charles . . . corroborate this with the police if asked?" I said.

"Yes."

"How long have you been seeing her?"

"On and off since grad school. But most recently, for about six months since last summer."

"You're an asshole."

"I'm not proud of it, if that means anything."

"It doesn't."

He continued speaking as if I hadn't interrupted him. "I plan to end it. Are you going to tell Val?" he asked as he looked up.

I ignored the question and didn't pursue his promise to end the affair. He had been lying to me and since I believed he'd continue to lie, I'd just be pissed off all the more. It already took all my control to keep from leaping over the desk and strangling him where he sat.

Plus, there were more questions.

"What about all that cash and a gun hidden away in the basement of the Catharine house?"

He shifted in the chair. It wasn't one of the gestures I had witnessed before when he lied.

"What money?"

"You renovated the house last year. You told me that. You don't know about the hidden panel in the basement?"

"Of course I know about the panel but no one else does," he said. "And nothing is behind it."

"Well, someone knows about it and hid cash and a weapon in there."

"You find anything else?"

"No. But I have to go to the police with this," I said.

"Really? Why?"

"Because I know. And if I don't, I could be named an accessory after the fact to a murder, and then charged with hindering a criminal investigation. And they would charge me, of that I have no doubt. They'd say if I weren't involved, I did it to help my brother-in-law, whom they will likely send to prison."

"Will you bring my name into it?" he asked.

"I think I can avoid that for the time being. But if I were you, I'd get a lawyer. Things like this can get messy, as if they aren't already."

Stuart looked at his telephone as if he were about to make the call. But he just put his elbows on his desk and locked his fingers together. He rested his chin on his fingers as he thought. But I had one more bombshell of a question to ask.

"Why would the mob be interested in a dead guy found in a house you own?"

"What? The mob? What have they got to do with anything?"

"That's what I'm asking you, Stuart," I said. "In the last two days, I've gotten visits from two mob factions — Patrese's and DelMarco's — both asking me who killed Henry Cummings."

"I'm telling you the truth, David. I don't know."

"You had better not know anything, otherwise one of

those guys'll come looking for you, and not to shake your hand," I said, pausing to let a dead seriousness descend. "And if one of them doesn't kill you, rest assured, I will."

CHAPTER XV

It was covered in blood

I got word to Chuckie, the bookie, to meet me in Center City, instead of up at Broad and Caleb where the gambling operation was headquartered. We met at a bar on 13th, just a half block north of City Hall. I knew the bartender there.

"What'll you have, Dave?" asked Imanu as he wiped down the bar.

"Nothing too strong. Just a beer should do it," I said.

"Coming right up," he said and went to the refrigerator behind the bar and brought out a long-neck brown bottle. In the effortless motion that could probably also be used to snap the neck of a small bird, he popped off the top and placed the bottle in front of me.

It was dark in the bar, well-suited for its location and its likely clientèle — city government bureaucrats and hard-drinking politicians thirsty for three-Martini lunches who didn't want to be easily recognized.

I was on a stool facing a large mirror behind the bar and saw Chuckie's reflection when he entered. Chuckie eased up to the bar next to me. Like my reporter friend Randolph, Chuckie must hate wearing an overcoat.

"What would you like to drink, Chuckie?" I asked. "I'm starting off with a beer."

"I need something stronger. I'll have a Scotch. Two fingers."

I motioned to Imanu, tapped the bar and he filled the order.

Once the drinks were in front of us, I lowered my voice and looked at his reflection as I spoke. He looked nervous and jittery, and I opted to not to turn to face him directly.

"So, what's going on?"

"New management wants to step things up," he said to my reflection. "Wants us to hustle more. Get more bets. They probably got more politicians to pay off just to stay in business. That happens whenever there's a new mayor. Always more mouths to feed in City Hall. Plus, there's more competition, with lottery machines coming into the area."

"What's the word on who killed Cummings?" I lifted my bottle and took a large gulp of beer.

"Some woman, maybe." He downed his Scotch and ordered another. A double. "Word on the street is that he was found naked."

I didn't verify that. "Any idea who?"

"Could be anybody. He got a lotta pussy. But he kept names to himself."

"Who's running things now?"

"Sammy. But not for long, I hear. Like I said, there's pressure from somewhere and it's not from Sammy. He's cool," Chuckie said, not bothering to fill me in on who Sammy was. I decided to come back to the subject later if I needed to. "Must be some silent partner Henry had. Everybody owes something to somebody else, you know."

"You hear anything else, you'll let me know?"

"As long as you're buying," Chuckie said, showing yellowed teeth as he smiled.

He took the last swallow of his drink and got up. I was astounded that a man of that size could drink that much alcohol. He didn't even stagger. I made a mental note never to get into a drinking contest with him.

~*~

I called Clara from a phone booth on the corner. She was in the office and about to head home. We hadn't talked and she wasn't pleased.

"What have you been doing?" she said impatiently.

"You know I'm working a couple of important cases," I replied.

"And you've been too busy to call me?"

"I'm sorry. I just got caught up in things. I'll make it up to you."

"How?"

I had to think quickly because I said it before I considered an answer and I didn't know what I'd do. I wasn't good at buying gifts for her — and she bought most of the gifts for me that I gave to others. She didn't care that much for candy and hated chocolates. Flowers would be good but I guessed, at the moment, they wouldn't be enough.

Before I made the call, I had been thinking about the Mafia and corruption in the Philadelphia/New Jersey region. More than anything else, the warring factions were seeking to control gambling, loan sharking and extortion in Atlantic City.

Then, in a flash of inspiration, it hit me.

Atlantic City.

"Why don't we get away. Just the two of us. For a weekend. We could head down to the shore on Friday afternoon and stay all weekend," I said. "What do you say? Let's get away this weekend."

She was quiet so I could tell the idea must have appealed to her. She was thinking it over. "No work?"

"No work. I promise," I said.

"If we come back too late, you'll miss Sunday night dinner with your dysfunctional family," she finally said.

I instantly knew what would sweeten and close the deal. "Okay, then, I'll tell you what. We stay through Sunday night and drive back Monday. Then I won't even be tempted to have dinner with them because there'd be no way I could. How's that?"

"Okay. Let's do it. You want to stay at the Sands? I could call Randall," she said.

Randall Wayne was another fraternity brother and old friend who was a manager at the hotel/casino and could get us a room even if the hotel was listed as being full.

"I'll call him," I said, "I need to talk to him anyway."

"You promised, Boo. Okay?" There was a pleading tone in her voice.

"I'll handle it right away. I promise."

"I love you. Thanks. You'll be over tonight?"

"I have work tonight but I'll call before I go to bed. Love you."

We hung up. I somehow had managed to please her without screwing up. But I knew I'd better call Randall as soon as I got back to my office.

~*~

Broad Street was a mess, as always. In the drive from City Hall to the city limits on the north there were more than two dozen traffic lights. Traffic was hell.

And totally unlike in South Philadelphia, cars in North Philadelphia were not allowed to park in the center median. It is illegal on both north and south Broad Street but since so many cops and powerful city politicians lived south, the police rarely issued tickets for cars parked in the center median in South Philadelphia.

I doubted it would change, now that the city had a Black mayor. After all, he didn't live in North Philadelphia, either. His home was in Overbrook.

I parked across the street from my office, as usual, and casually looked around for any police photographers taking my picture. Not that I could have done anything about it if they had been. I might pose a little to show them I knew they were there but it was more useful to me for them to think I was unaware. That's Counter-surveillance 101.

The office was dark. Centerton had left for the day. I switched on the lights and went to my little office.

Sitting down, I went into the desk and pulled out an address book. Finding the number, I called the Sands Hotel and Casino in Atlantic City.

"Randall, it's Snooopy Dog. How you doing?"

"I'm good, Dave. How are you?"

"Getting by."

He got to the point, although I was the one making the call. "You want a room?"

"Yeah," I replied. "This weekend. For three nights, starting Friday, if possible."

"Ocean view?"

"Of course, if you can swing it."

"You coming down alone or will Clara be with you?"

Since Randall and Clara were friends, I would never ask him for a room if I was taking a woman other than Clara. I may not know where my relationship with Clara was going — or even if I wanted it to go there — but I would never cheat on her.

I'm not my brother-in-law.

"We'll be together," I said.

"I'll check availability and call you back. Where are you?"

"My office. You have the number."

"I'll call you back in a couple of minutes."

"Randall, just another minute," I said quickly, stopping him from ending the call. "Uh, have you . . . uh . . . have you seen or talk to Raymond Dawson lately?"

His answer came rather slowly, like an invisible force was pulling it out of him. "Yeah. Last week. At an event up in Philly," he said. "Why you ask?"

I didn't answer that but started for the heart of the matter. "Have you met his girlfriend?"

Randall paused as if to think, perhaps to consider how much to tell me. "Audrey. Yeah. They're engaged."

"You know anything else?"

"What are you getting at, David? Fishing for gossip?"

"No. Absolutely not," I stammered ahead. The phone receiver felt heavy in my hand.

"She's pregnant, if that's what you're getting at," he said.

Now it was my turn to pause and think. In truth, I had been considering this call to Randall ever since I took Ray's case.

"Listen, Bulldog," I pleaded, using his fraternity name. I hoped it would remind him of a sacred bond we pledged together as frat brothers years ago. "I need to keep this between us."

He acknowledged that bond by simply saying, "Go on."

"Is there any reason to believe . . . that Audrey's baby . . . isn't Raymond's? I can't go into any details, but it's for a case."

He was quick in his response, which surprised me but probably shouldn't have.

"He came to you, didn't he? What a jackass," Randall said firmly. "I told him it was useless when he mentioned it to me when I saw him."

"You knew?" I said.

"Of course. For several months. We keep in touch."

Raymond and I had been so close back in the day that not knowing this bit of important information sooner was embarrassing.

"Look," Randall continued. "He's just scared of the commitment, just like you . . . with Clara." He stopped to let that sink in. "Raymond's looking for a possible way out, is my guess. That's got to be why he came to you. But believe me, it's his."

"Good," I said, hoping he couldn't hear my relief.

"And you know how we can tell?" he said.

"No. How?' I was curious.

"He's AB-negative," Randall said. "You know that? He told me some time ago. It's one of the rarest blood types. Fewer than five percent of the worldwide population have that blood type. If his newborn is AB-negative, that's the ball game for Raymond."

He returned to the original reason for our conversation. "I'll call you back in a few minutes about the room."

And he hung up.

~*~

It didn't take long for Randall to call me back. He got an ocean-view room for two nights — and at a considerable discount — but it wouldn't be for another day before he could confirm the room for the third night. He suggested I call again in the morning. I really needed the room for Sunday night but at least I had accomplished something that would likely please Clara, I told him.

While Randall and I shared a history as frat brothers, I think the glue that currently held us together — and that provided a certain amount of friction — was Clara. They were friends, close friends, and had been for years. Though I doubt Clara noticed and Randall would deny it if questioned, he suffered with an unrequited love for her that, our mutual frat brother Raymond once told me, developed years ago when Randall first met Clara, which was before I met her.

He was built like a modern-day Apollo, muscular with a broad chest and shoulders, a narrow waist, and well-sculptured thighs that were perfect for running or helping to lift heavy objects.

Unfortunately for him, he was not handsome. Far from it.

He had kind eyes and a soft-spoken manner, which women love, but also an oddly shaped head that was too small for his body.

According to Raymond, Clara instantly, though not harshly, shot him down when Randall finally worked up the courage to ask her out. Once I was on the scene, he always reminded me to treat her right, as she deserved. It's why he'd bend over backwards to help me if he felt it also benefited her.

It made my decision to get a room at the shore an easier one. And after agreeing to call him back the next day, it was easy to fall asleep when I got home.

Less than an inch of snow fell overnight, and it left a heavy coating of wet snow on cars and grassy surfaces. I had considered calling Thompson with the news of the hidden panel in the Catharine Street house but decided against it. I'd do it in person.

I got there just as O'Donnell and Thompson were walking in. "Thompson," I said, "I need to talk. It's about the Henry Cummings case."

"You need me for this?" O'Donnell asked. He didn't care for me or for my presence regarding the Cummings case. And while he tried to stay neutral when I was present, his irritation was always just below the surface.

"No, that's all right, Johnny," Thompson said, indicating where he wanted me to sit as O'Donnell walked off. "It's probably nothing. Just some bullshit from a bull-shitter." He took a chair and got something to write on. "Okay, hotshot, what've you got?"

"There's money and a gun hidden away behind a secret panel in the basement at the house on Catharine."

"Ah-uh. And you know that how?"

"You aren't going to like this," I said.

"Oh, I'm sure of that," he said, studying me closely. "But go on."

"I snuck in the house yesterday and looked around while you and everyone else was at the scene of that mob hit."

"That's breaking and entering, you know. It's illegal. I could have you arrested," he said, inhaling deeply then letting it go.

"Not in this case, detective, and you know it. I have a key," I added pointedly. "Nothing about it indicated it was still an active crime scene."

Thompson didn't argue the point but wasn't letting me off the hook just yet. "You touch anything, contaminate any evidence?"

"No didn't leave any prints. I used a handkerchief if I touched anything."

Thompson scratched behind his left ear and took some notes with his right hand. Glancing up at me, "Why tell me this now? Maybe you planted it there."

"No, and you know it. It's an interior wall facing the furnace."

"You expect me to take your word . . . that it's there?"

"Believe it or not. That's up to you."

Thompson scooted back in the chair and put his hands behind his head. "Whose money is it?"

"No idea."

"You mess up anything in that house and I'll have you for obstruction and tampering with evidence of a crime. I mean it."

"I'm well aware," I said.

"Get out of here and go complicate someone else's life."

~*~

I was on a payphone on Broad and Walnut confirming with Randall my weekend getaway with Clara — and he threw in a third night's stay — when I turned around and there, standing far too close, was Big Sally. I didn't know how long he had been there but he certainly could have hurt me, even possibly killed me, before I was aware of any danger.

"Thanks, Randall," I said, eyeing the mobster but keeping the conversation short. I hung up.

"You going on a vacation this weekend? Good for you," he said with a nasty smile on his ugly, pock-marked face. His cheeks looked like Swiss cheese.

"What do you want?" I said, standing my ground.

"Boss wants an update on the investigation."

"He'll have to wait," I said

"The boss don't like ta wait," he said, grabbing my arm with the force of a vice grip. He looked over toward a car illegally idling at the curb, though it didn't appear that someone was inside. I guess I was going to take a ride.

"Is there a problem, gentlemen?" asked a large police officer mounted on a horse who happened by.

Big Sally looked up and eased his grip, then let go altogether.

"No, officer," I said, once again eyeing the mobster. "My friend here just discovered some coins I left in the bottom of the pay phone and was giving them back to me."

The officer looked back and forth between us with suspicion but let it drop. To Big Sally, he said, "You might want to move your vehicle. It's illegally parked."

Big Sally said nothing and went back to his car, getting in on the driver's side and heading out.

"Buddy," the officer said, once the mobster was gone. "You should be a little more careful about losing your coins. That gentleman," the officer nodded his head in the direction of the departing car, "and others like him, don't take 'No' easily."

With that, he slowly rode off.

~*~

I was in my office for most of the rest of the day, working my cases on the telephone with various sources, and placing a small ad in a local weekly community newspaper advertising for new clients.

The ride home in the Mustang was uneventful. I thought about my confrontation with Big Sally and how it might go the next time around. I wondered why both factions were so interested in Cummings' murder. Yes, it was in South Philadelphia, where they operated most extensively, and I doubted they'd be as concerned if it happened up north.

But I thought there was more to it than just that.

I found a space around the corner from my apartment and walked back. Though it was dark, I noticed something with fuzzy sunshine yellow hair off in the bushes to the right of the steps of the apartment building. Then, it jumped out at me. It was a clown that wore a menacing smirk under extremely heavy face makeup, yellow hair, black leather gloves and a tight, black jumpsuit.

And he had a knife in his hand.

Nearly before I had a chance to react, he lunged at me. I moved back fast as the blade sliced toward my coat. The attacker failed to contact but he recovered and approached again. I jumped back onto the sidewalk, keeping as much distance between us as possible and never taking my eyes off the knife. Identifying my attacker would have to come later.

I was taller and with a fuller build. But I was at a distinct disadvantage because I was wearing a wool jacket, while my attacker wore a more maneuverable jumpsuit. His exhaled breath swirled in the chilly February air but since we were both being driven by adrenaline, it was unlikely the mercury had much impact on either of us.

I was trained in hand-to-hand combat in my Naval intelligence unit and it was being put to good use. Though agile, this knife-wielding clown was not a natural at it. He was flat-footed and his attack was clumsy and unfocused. He slashed back and forth in a way that, while dangerous, was easy to escape if the victim had any real training, which I had.

After he made one slashing motion to my right, I reached forward with my left hand and grabbed his wrist. Twisting in the opposite direction, I lifted the arm up and away. My attacker jammed a foot into my right shin and I let out a cry in pain, falling back and letting go of the clown's wrist.

He came at me again, but I was able to grab his arm and spin him around. He dropped the knife and I held him close to my body. He was smaller than I originally thought and not nearly as muscular. I could smell him, we were so close, and his body odor was sweeter than I would have thought. As I was about to grab the yellow wig with my free hand, a sharp elbow hit me in the right side. I doubled over in intense, nearly unbearable pain, and my hand reached for my side.

The knife had already fallen off into the darkness and, not seeing it, my attacker melted into the night.

The elbow to the side was hard but I didn't understand why my side hurt so much until I bought my hand up.

It was covered in blood.

I staggered into the street and tried to flag down a car. The first one, seeing a bleeding Black man in the street, sped off. Shock was starting to set in and I was about to faint when a second car approached. It stopped. The driver was a middle-aged white guy with snow white hair. I told him what happened. Then, I passed out.

CHAPTER XVI

When they left, I was blessedly alone.

The nearest hospital, Pennsylvania Presbyterian, was less than a mile away. I woke up in a recovery room, a large bandage strapped across my midsection, and with Thompson and O'Donnell standing over me.

"That's a nasty cut, Blaise," Thompson said, sounding genuinely concerned.

I tried to move but thought better of it as pain swept over me.

"Can he tell us what happened?" O'Donnell asked a doctor in a white lab coat and a nurse in blue standing to the left. I hadn't noticed them at first.

The doctor was a petite young woman with olive skin and long, jet black hair. Judging from what was stitched on a patch on her jacket, her last name was Guaygua. I couldn't read the name tag on the nurse, a tall, powerfully built man with tattoos running down his right arm. He looked like he'd be ready for any emergency, medical or otherwise. They both looked down at me with guarded concern.

"Yes, he can talk," the doctor finally said to the officers. To me, she said, "But I want you to lie still and don't move. I don't want you tearing anything open. We do good work here."

That was a stupid statement. Lying still implies not moving. It's redundant, I thought. *But why am I thinking about grammar after being stitched up in the hospital?*

I nodded my agreement to the doctor, who petted my shoulder and left with the nurse. They closed the partition.

"What happened?" O'Donnell said

I spoke and was surprised that my voice was so hoarse. I apologized for it as I described the attack and the attacker, searching my memory without success for more details.

They wrote it all down in little notebooks as I spoke.

"Sorry I can't remember more," I said with irritation.

"No problem, Blaise," O'Donnell said, though I wasn't sure he meant it.

"From what you've said, this doesn't look like a simple mugging, though I think someone wanted it to look that way," Thompson said. "Someone doesn't like you. Any idea who?"

"Not really. But haven't had time to think much about it," I said. "You find the weapon?"

"Still canvassing the area," O'Donnell said. "I personally checked the immediate area when I was up there."

"I've got to start carrying a piece," I said.

"Wouldn't have done you much good, given the speed your assailant appeared and attacked you," Thompson said. "When someone gets within about twenty feet of you before you can pull out a weapon, having a gun is generally useless. I wish more people who carry a gun knew that."

"You're right. I wouldn't have had the time to aim and fire."

"Anyone you want us to call for you?" Thompson asked.

"A girlfriend, maybe?" O'Donnell said.

"I'll get my sister or her husband. They can take me home once I'm released," I said, stopping to quickly think of what lay ahead. "Damn. I'm supposed to go away this weekend with my lady. I can't back out of it now."

"You're in no shape to go anywhere," Thompson said, putting away his notebook. He and his partner walked to the partition, pulling it aside.

"Yeah but you getting out of Philadelphia may do you some good. Keep you out of harm's way . . . and out of our hair," O'Donnell said. Just before he pulled the curtain shut and the officers left, O'Donnell added, "Have a good time in Atlantic City. Lay low and rest. And leave the policing to the professionals."

Once they were gone, I closed my eyes and quietly let time pass. I might have even drifted off to sleep when the partition suddenly opened and Dr. Guaygua entered. She walked over to the monitors hooked up to my body, studied the readouts on the screens, and then looked down at me.

She was as thin as she was young, which in both instances was quite a lot, and had deep brown eyes that were reassuring despite her youth. She reached for the stethoscope around her neck and put the earpieces in her ears.

"Stay still. I'm going to listen to your heart," she said, placing the chest piece to my body with her small, delicate hands. She intensely examined one side of my chest, and then the other before replacing the stethoscope around her neck.

"How's it sound?" I inquired.

"You're alive," the doctor said with a wry smile, though dodging the question. "How are you feeling? Your pain level."

"Some pain but tolerable," I said as I mentally assessed the different parts of my body to see what was working.

"I could get you stronger meds if you're hurting," she said. "No need to needlessly suffer."

"No, I'm good."

She looked down at me with those searching brown eyes.

"You're lucky. You were injured on the right side, not too deep and away from internal organs. None were perforated, despite the blood loss," Dr. Guaygua said.

"How serious is it?" I asked. "And when can I go home?" I moved as if to get up and then stopped. "Ahhh. Now that hurts."

She displayed a slight Mona Lisa smile at my comical effort to get out of bed. "Just lie still," Dr. Guaygua said, placing her hands deep into her lab coat. "You'll fully recover in time, if you rest, though you'll probably have a slight scar. But it, too, will fade in time.

"But because you were unconscious when you arrived, I'd like to keep you overnight for observation. Just as a precaution," she said. "Your heart sounds good but you lost a nice amount of blood, which is why you passed out. I assume it was from shock. However, I just want to be sure. I'm admitting you. They'll take you up to a room soon."

Though I didn't want to stay, I accepted it. I stopped her as she turned to leave.

"Thank you, doctor," I said weakly.

"It's no problem. I'll come up to check on you a little later once you're settled."

~*~

Dr. Guaygua stopped in to check on me twice during the night and signed the release papers in the morning. I couldn't imagine the hours she was putting in.

Stuart and Valerie came the next morning to get me, with Val walking beside the orderly pushing the wheelchair out the front entrance to the waiting car for the ride home. I was stiff but required little assistance getting into the front passenger seat of the car. Once I was inside and settled, Valerie got in the back and Stuart drove.

Probably because of the drugs, I nodded off on the short ride to my apartment, and once inside, Valerie fussed about while Stuart remained stoic.

The light was blinking on the answering machine beside the bed. It was probably Clara, but I just didn't have the energy, so I ignored it.

I had a moment alone with Stuart as my sister was in the kitchen doing heaven knows what.

I whispered when I spoke.

"We need to talk," I said.

"Do you think this . . . your attack . . . has anything to do with my case?"

"I don't know, but I plan to get to the bottom of things," I said.

Valerie returned to the bedroom with a tray and a bowl of chicken soup, placing it on my lap as I sat up in bed.

"You need to eat," she said in a stern voice that mimicked our grandmother.

"Not hungry. I just got stabbed last night, remember. In the abdomen."

"Yes, and the nice lady doctor said it wasn't that deep despite the blood. You need your strength, so eat. We aren't leaving here until you do," she said.

I had no doubt she meant it. Valerie was in full Momma Bear mode. Then something occurred to me.

"Shouldn't both of you be at work? And who's watching the kids?"

"School," Valerie said, making sure the blanket was comfortable around me and that the tray of food was easily accessible.

Not wanting them to remain any longer than possible, and certainly not any longer than Stuart was prepared to stay, I picked up the spoon and took a sip — and nearly dropped it back into the bowl.

"Too hot?" she said, noticing my reaction.

"You think?" I responded. But I grabbed the spoon again and scooped up more soup, blowing ripples across the liquid to cool it off. I took a tentative mouthful, sucking a noodle through my lips and down my throat.

"I don't want either of you to mention this to Clara. You hear me? Not a word. She has enough to worry about," I instructed.

"Why not? She's your girlfriend. She deserves to know," my sister said, striking a pose with her hands on her hips.

"I mean it. Not a word. It's my decision and I'll tell her in my own way and in my own time. End of story. And not Grammy Taylor, either. Not a word from either of you. I'll talk to them when the time is right."

Valerie turned away without saying another word and grabbed her coat, which was in a chair near the bedroom door. Returning to the bed, she leaned over me and kissed my forehead.

"Get some rest and I'll check in on you this evening and bring you some dinner," she said. "But if you need anything before then, you call me and I'll be right over. You understand?"

"Yes, I get it," was my weak reply.

"And Mrs. Findley has my number, too."

Stuart said nothing and just nodded his agreement with whatever Valerie said.

When they left, I was blessedly alone.

~*~

With the pain meds, I rested surprisingly well throughout the day. Valerie stopped by in the evening to fuss over me and to bring a light dinner. But when she left, I went back to sleep easily.

I woke early, got up, and turned on the television after a quick trip to the bathroom to relieve myself, and to check and change my dressing. I felt stiff but wasn't as uncomfortable as I would have thought.

I rarely watch early morning television but since I was convalescing, what else was I to do? I turned on The Today Show but the national broadcast was in a local news break.

A pretty blonde named Jennifer Something-Or-Another was at the anchor desk reading a serious news story, though the morning audience probably preferred something lighter.

"A city police spokeswoman said the nail bomb exploded just as the victim reached his front door. It sent nails, debris, and the victim's shattered and shredded body back all the way to the street. The explosion destroyed the porch of the house and much of the interior on the first floor.

"The victim was identified as thirty-two-year-old Mario Stazzia of the Thirteen-hundred block of Federal Avenue in South Philadelphia. Because of the explosion and the police and fire department activity that followed, traffic was blocked on Broad Street for much of the night and the Broad Street Subway line was halted. SEPTA used shuttle buses to ferry people around the area. The street was reopened and subway service resumed just before the start of the morning rush," Jennifer Something-Or-Another said, trying to look serious.

"Stazzia was reputedly a mob associate, most recently linked to reputed Mafia leader Michele 'Mikie' DelMarco," she said. The camera focused on images on the screen behind her, causing me to briefly shudder. "Stazzia can be seen here in a clown suit during a party DelMarco held at Children's Hospital last Christmas for kids with cancer."

My mind shifted to the present. Could that dead guy in the clown suit, Stazzia, have been my attacker? But just as quickly as the question formed in my head the answer came back, no. The DelMarco faction had never threatened me and Stazzia would have had ample opportunity before last night if they had. Plus, and most importantly, he was a big man. My attacker was a much smaller man, if my memory served me correctly.

My attention returned to the TV.

"There have been nearly two dozen mob assassinations in or around Philadelphia since mob boss Angelo Bruno was killed in 1980. We will have more details on this latest killing on Action News at noon," she said, turning to a smiling and cheerful weatherman, who didn't appear to have heard a thing the news anchor just read on-air.

I took a moment to absorb the news. Stazzia was the driver of DelMarco's car. So, in less than a week, mob hits had touched both warring factions.

~*~

I felt pretty good and despite my doctor's orders — and my sister's insistence — I was determined to get out. I called Allison Charles' office shortly after 9 a.m. and didn't expect to reach her directly, but the call was patched through.

"Good morning, Miss Charles. It's David Blaise. I was hoping to have a word with you this morning."

There was a pause and I could nearly hear a clock ticking in her head. "Sure. What time?"

"Ten-thirty?"

"Can't that soon. Let me look at my calendar for a second," she said, followed by a moment of silence. "I'll change some things around and can be free at lunchtime. How's that?"

"Fine. Where? Your office?"

"No," she said. The response was quick. "I don't want you up in my office again but I want this finished. How about neutral territory? Do you know the Valley Green Inn?"

"Yes. Off Henry Avenue back in the woods along the Wissahickon Creek."

"I'll meet you there at noon. I'm busy and have very limited time. Don't be late."

~*~

Fairmount Park in Philadelphia, which was added to the National Registry of Historic Places in 1972, just as I joined the Navy, is the largest municipal park in the country. It's not a contiguous park, and thus not all sections intersect. However, it covers thousands of acres of land across the city. It's estimated that fifty percent of the city's 1.5 million people live within two miles of some section of Fairmount Park.

One section includes Wissahickon Valley Park in northwest Philadelphia. It's dominated by heavy woods, and walking and riding trails. It seems so remote that it's hard to believe it's still in one of the largest cities in the United States.

The Valley Green Inn is located in a wooded area adjoining the Wissahickon, a narrow creek that spills into the Schuylkill

River, and is upstream from a stone arch bridge. It's so remote and pristine it would be a great place to hide a body . . . if your motives were sinister. I surmised, however, that Allison's motives had more to do with privacy — and not being seen with me — than with anything else.

I grimaced as I pulled on my pants. Getting into a shirt was torture but I managed. While I had a Glock in my office, I kept a small Smith and Wesson revolver in the kitchen cabinet. I slipped it into my jacket pocket on the way out.

There were no suspicious cars with mobsters in them parked outside and I didn't see any clowns as I made my way to the car. The drive to our meeting place was equally uneventful.

The restaurant looked like an old white country inn with hunter green shutters. In warmer weather, there were tables on its porch, which stretched from one end of the front of the building to the other.

The setting was rustic and comfortable. I was seated at a table with a tablecloth that was starched so white it made the table look like it was covered in snow. I was looking out the window when I saw Allison walk up the front steps and enter the restaurant.

Allison looked around before spotting me. She came over and, as a gentleman, I should have stood up. But I didn't. She took the chair opposite me after taking off her coat and placing it on the back of her chair. She was business casual — a light fabric coat in black wool over a smart pair of charcoal gray slacks and matching sweater.

Our water glasses were already filled, and she grabbed hers, took a sip and put it back down.

"Let's just get this over with. What do you want?"

While the restaurant wasn't empty, it wasn't very busy yet. The nearest occupied table was some distance away. But still, I kept my voice low.

"I know some things about your relationship with Stuart Thomas and I know some things that he told me were lies. I was hoping you could clarify some . . . inconsistencies."

"Why should I help you?" she said.

"Because I'd like to resolve this thing before the police get involved and start asking you questions." I said. "I have talked to the police, of course, but I've kept both of you out of the conversation."

"I still don't see why I should help you. You're still gonna burn us both."

"If I wanted to do that, I would have already."

The waitress arrived to take our orders. Allison might have needed to get it over with quickly but I was hungry, so I ordered a walnut and apple salad and a crab cake sandwich. Allison ordered just the Inn Salad and coffee.

"My client in this case," I said after the waitress left, "is Stuart Thomas. The day after the killing, he asked me to look into who killed Henry Cummings at the house his firm quietly owns."

"I know that all already. He told me."

"Did he also mention that I'm his brother-in-law?" I said, waiting for a reaction. Her eyebrows inched up into her forehead but she didn't say anything. "Yes, the man you're screwing is married to my sister."

The waitress returned with Allison's coffee and both our salads. We continued to talk as we ate.

"I didn't know that," she said, spearing a small portion of lettuce and a crouton and placing it in her mouth. She chewed like a proper lady, barely moving her jaw. But then, the portion was small.

"Now you might understand why I'd like to keep this hush-hush."

"Okay. I understand. To protect your family," she said casually as she added sugar to her coffee and stirred the dark fluid. Steam was rising from the fine-bone China coffee cup.

"I think Stuart is an asshole. I've told him that. But I'm not here to pass judgment. On you or him. I'm just trying to save my sister from embarrassment, and if possible keep him out of jail," I said. "What I need are some answers and to know why he's lied to me. He originally told me he was out of town . . . in Harrisburg . . . on the night Cummings was killed. Then, he confessed to being with you all night. Which is it?"

"He said he was with me?" she said before taking more food.

"In your townhouse? All night?"

"Let me think. Yeah, that's right. He was there."

My sandwich arrived but I wasn't immediately interested in eating, though the food was superb.

"Now you're lying. I checked your calendar. And yes, I have sources that got me that information. You were out of town, in Manhattan, that day. At a fundraiser for Ed Rendell. You were scheduled to take Amtrak's Metroliner back the next day."

It had been a while since she had touched either the salad or the coffee. Now she was wringing her hands.

"I like Stu. I always have. He's sweet and considerate. And yes, I know he's married and is never going to leave his wife. But I only want a small piece of him. I'm willing to accept what little he can give me."

It was utter bullshit — a lie this woman was willing to say to herself to justify sleeping with another woman's man.

Allison Charles had it all together for the outside — professional success, some manner of financial security, and loads of nice clothes. She was an extremely stylish and put-together woman.

On the outside.

But on the inside, I thought she was confused, vulnerable and insecure. The question was whether she was willing to possibly perjure herself for a married man, even one whom she confessed to like.

I considered that as I ate.

"When I heard about Henry on the news that morning when I got back from New York, I knew at once which house it was in . . . Stuart's townhouse on Catharine. I called Stu at the office to ask what happened. He sounded nervous. He denied doing anything to Henry. But I wasn't sure I believed him. He didn't like Henry, never had. Not since I introduced them."

I was bringing the sandwich up to my mouth but stopped. A thought struck me. She called Cummings by his first name, and in a way someone speaks of a person they know well.

"You introduced them?" I said. "How did you know Henry Cummings?"

"I know what you must already think of me. But look at it from my perspective. It's really difficult to meet successful Black men in this town," she said, looking at her water and tracing her finger around the rim of the glass. She didn't pick it up as she continued talking. "Most of the men are married. Of the ones that aren't, well, they generally feel threatened by a strong successful woman who doesn't need them for anything."

Well, you need us for some things, I see. You were having an affair with at least one, and possibly with two.

I was glad I didn't voice that observation. Even the thought was judgmental.

"So the only men available who aren't threatened by a woman's success are either poor, gay, in jail or married. And not all of them fit the bill," she continued.

"I met Henry at a function several years ago. And he was such a charming man. Stu is sweet and attentive, but Henry was charming. Incredibly charming. Henry asked for my number but I wouldn't give it to him. I was working at the Port Authority and he knew that. It was easy for him to find me. Within a week, I was getting flowers and notes from him sent to the office."

"You didn't tell him to stop it?" I said.

"No. I wasn't seeing Stu at the time, and . . . in time . . . Henry and I started talking and struck up a friendship," she said. "First one thing, then another, and soon Henry and I were lovers. I didn't intend for it to happen but it did. And like I said, Stu wasn't in the picture at the time."

I was totally intrigued by her story and, in fact, by her. I could see why men were drawn to her. She was beautiful and sexy. And she had a quality about her I couldn't name.

"I was at an event on the riverfront and Stu was there and Henry was there, and I introduced them. Stu assumed I was with Henry, though it was over with Henry by then. But Stu gets jealous. Extremely jealous. He called me the next night and then showed up at the house. He was crazy mad. I tried to calm him down, to assure him nothing was going on between Henry and me. Not anymore. But he wouldn't listen. Even when Stu and I started seeing each other again, any time Henry's name came up, Stu would blow his stack. I was sure if he ever saw Henry again, Stu would try to hurt him. That's why I lied just now. I wanted to protect Stu, just like you're trying to do with him and his family. Your family."

"But do you think Stu is capable of murder?"

"I don't know. He certainly hated Henry enough," she said. "And after all, Henry was killed in Stu's townhouse."

"Why would he be there?"

"I don't know. I have no idea how he got in there," she said.

"So why did you go there, to the house, the next day? I saw you." I said.

"You really were in the house . . . hiding . . . and saw me?"

"You came up to the third floor and went left, toward the bedroom. Like I told you before, I was hiding to the right of the stairs," I said.

"Behind the door to the roof," she said.

"Yes. I got in the same way as you. From the patio in back. I guess we both left the same way."

"I wanted to see what had happened and to see if Stu left anything to incriminate himself. I went to protect him," she said. "I can see how Henry might want to stick it to Stu because of me. They were both competitive like that. I can see how Henry might take someone to the house for sex knowing Stu would figure out someone . . . like Henry, in this case . . . used Stu's secret hideaway. Stu probably went there, saw Henry, confronted him, and . . . " she stopped before the words traveled over her lips.

I completed the thought for her.

"Killed him."

CHAPTER XVII

The itch in the middle of my back.

Allison's description of events made sense, certainly enough sense that Stuart could be brought in by the police for questioning. And given his lack of alibi, it might be enough for his arrest. Perhaps.

And yet, I couldn't quite see the man who sat at my grandmother's dining room table on Sunday evenings as a killer, despite what other secrets he held. Just because Allison said it didn't mean all of it, or any of it, was true. With so much on the line for her life and her career, I was sure she'd be willing to lie her pretty ass off.

Plus, there was something else. Something about her unsettled me. I couldn't put my finger on it, but something was there, like an itch in the middle of the back, the very place between the shoulder blades that no matter how hard I tried, I couldn't reach. I had seen her up close three times and each time was slightly different.

What was it about her? What made her the itch in the middle of my back?

~*~

On the way back downtown, I called Stuart. It was time to address some things again — man-to-man. Like with Allison, I preferred a quiet, out of the way place. But there wasn't the time to arrange it, so it wasn't an option.

"I can be in Suburban Station in thirty minutes," I said. "There's a coffee shop near the ticket windows. At this time in the afternoon, we can get a quiet table near the back of the shop. I'll meet you there."

I returned down Henry Avenue into the city, finally reaching East River Drive along the Schuylkill River. Around the Art Museum, I headed down Ben Franklin Parkway into Center City. Miraculously, I found an open parking spot on Market Street, just outside a porno bookstore, which was sandwiched between a haberdashery and a men's hat store.

I was in a busy area in Center City with lots of foot and vehicular traffic. Good to stay in the open if I was being followed.

The Suburban Station was a block over in the opposite direction and I reached the coffee shop before Stuart. I took a booth, ordered coffee, and waited. It was lukewarm by the time he showed. After he sat down, I motioned for a waitress in a white dress and red and white apron to come over. "Could you refresh this for me?" I said, handing her the cup. To Stuart, I said, "You want anything?"

"I'll have a large cup. Sugar, no cream."

She left to fill the order.

"I just got back from lunch," I said.

"How wonderful that you can handle such a difficult task alone," he said.

"I wasn't alone, Stuart. And you won't be so snide once you hear what I just learned."

He eyed me smugly. "Okay. Enlighten me."

The waitress returned with a cup in each hand, and placed Stuart's fresh cup in front of him. "The packets are on the table," the waitress said and left.

I got the little silver pitcher of cream sitting on the table and added some to my hot cup. It swirled and turned the dark brown coffee into a mocha color.

"So," he said again, "enlighten me."

"Your alibi doesn't hold up with what Allison Charles just told me. She says you weren't at her place that night. The night of the Cummings murder. In fact, she claims to have been in

Manhattan. Her office calendar supports that. I checked."

Stuart, who was pouring sugar into his coffee, seemed taken aback. His eyes shifted quickly right to left several times as if he'd find the answer to his next statement from inside his coffee. "She's lying," he finally said in a hushed voice but not directly to me.

"And why's that?"

"I have no idea why she'd lie, but we were there. Together," he said, looking down as he stirred, then back to me.

"Without her, you have no alibi. You weren't home. We know that. You weren't in Harrisburg as you told me earlier and you apparently weren't with Allison. You have no alibi," I said. "So, the question remains, where were you that night?"

He took a napkin from the dispenser, wiped his hands with it and then wiped the table in front of him, although I didn't see where he had spilled any coffee. He hadn't even picked up the coffee yet.

"I shouldn't need any alibi," he said.

"That is not how the police will look at it. Since it . . . the murder . . . occurred in a house your company owns, the police may want to know where you were," I said. "In addition, if they interview Allison, you certainly are gonna need an alibi."

"What? Why?"

"Allison can provide a motive for you. And it's a powerful one."

"Motive? What motive? For what?"

"Jealousy."

He nearly stood up in the booth. "Jealousy? What in God's name of?"

I looked around to see if we were drawing a crowd or any attention. I reached across the table to grab Stuart's wrist. "Calm down and sit. And keep your voice down."

He took a couple of deep breaths and quieted.

"Allison said when you resumed your affair with her, you became extremely jealous of her affair with Cummings, although they were no longer seeing each other. She says you were so enraged it frightened her."

"That's not true. I didn't even know she knew the man until a few weeks ago. And she never mentioned an affair. Jealousy. That's just insane," he protested a little too loudly but it didn't appear to attract anyone else's attention.

"That's not what I heard," I said, and sipped some coffee.

"What you heard is wrong," Stuart said. "Allison wasn't sleeping with Cummings. At least I don't think so. She never mentioned it. She owed him money. And I think it was a lot."

Now I was surprised. "What? She owed Henry Cummings money? The numbers guy?"

"Allison came to me a few weeks ago . . . maybe six weeks. I don't exactly remember. Said she was in some sort of trouble. And I thought, uh-oh, she's pregnant," he said.

"Was she?" I asked quickly, fearing the possible answer.

"No, that wasn't it," Stuart said, apparently unaware of my discomfort. "She said she had been doing some illegal gambling . . . numbers stuff . . . and she was in debt. She needed money. Fast."

Stuart looked up as a couple of older people wandered close by before taking a nearby booth. They didn't seem to notice us, but I lowered my voice to a near whisper when I spoke. Stuart had to lean in close to hear me.

"How much?"

"I don't know. She didn't say. But she wanted to know if I could get her some cash."

"And did you? Give her some money?" I took another swallow of my coffee.

"No. A couple of days later, she came to me to say whatever problems she was having were resolved. She apparently got the money somewhere else."

"She say where?"

"No, and I didn't ask," he said. "You've seen her. She's high maintenance. The woman loves clothes. And shoes. She has a nice car and an expensive house. I have no idea how she maintains all that but it's not because of me."

"I'm supposed to believe that?" I said.

"Yes, because it's true," he responded. "Oh yeah, I've bought her nice things from time to time. Baubles here and there. But . . . our relationship . . . is mostly physical. We get together for sex. That's generally it. We're two highly successful, professional people. We don't need each other's money. At least I didn't think so."

"She was into Cummings for money. Huh," I said, mostly to myself. I was looking out into the station, watching people scurry off to their trains.

Stuart had barely touched the coffee.

"I think so," he said.

"She said she originally claimed you were with her to protect you, to provide you with an alibi in case you needed it," I said. "Now that's gone. And it's her word against yours. You weren't seen that night and there's no way of proving she owed Henry Cummings money. I'm sure his numbers running operation isn't going to open up the books to the government and say, 'See, she owed us money.'"

"It's why she came to me. She couldn't afford for anyone to find out she was playing the numbers," he said.

"Stuart, I'm trying to keep this on the down-low. But once the police start snooping, there's no telling what they may find. You've got to get a lawyer, and a good one," I said. "And you should consider telling Valerie. If you treasure her and your kids . . . and I can't believe I'm about to say this but I know you do treasure them . . . you have to prepare them for it. You don't want it to blow up in their faces."

~*~

If there was ever a time when I needed help sorting things out it was now. But where to turn?

I called Randolph at the office from a pay phone in Suburban Station and we agreed to meet at his favorite drinking hole — how surprising? — in 20 minutes. Since I was still parked downtown, I knew it wouldn't be a long walk.

But as I reached the tavern, a police squad car pulled up and out stepped O'Donnell. Thompson was in the driver's seat. "We'd like to have a chat, Blaise. Get in the car," O'Donnell said in a no nonsense tone. I knew it was unwise to resist.

I got in back; O'Donnell got in the front. We were parked in a No Parking zone but they didn't seem in a hurry to move. We just sat there.

O'Donnell, the junior officer of the two, remained facing forward while Thompson turned in his seat to face me. He didn't look happy. I had been holding back pieces of information from them from the beginning, providing only as much as I felt I could get away with. And I knew that approach could, and probably would, come back to haunt me.

It appeared the day had come.

"We've been looking for you, and got a tip you'd be down this way," O'Donnell said, though not elaborating on where the tip came from.

"After searching one shell company after another, we finally found out who actually owns the house on Catharine where Henry Cummings was murdered," Thompson said. "You want to venture a guess as to who it is, Blaise?"

"I feel pretty confident he won't have to guess," O'Donnell said while still facing forward. I didn't say anything, never taking an eye from Thompson. O'Donnell looked at his partner. "You know, maybe he doesn't know and we *should* tell him," he said, finally turning partially back to me. "It's the Stuart Thomas Real Estate Development Company."

"And who's the principal owner? Stuart Thomas. And after a little more digging, do you know what we discovered?" Thompson said. "That you're related to Stuart Thomas. His wife is *your* sister. Imagine THAT."

"Yes," I admitted. "He's my brother-in-law."

"Bingo," O'Donnell said.

"I told you to stay out of the way. But I also told you if you had any relevant information about this case, you were to bring it to me," Thompson said, adding, "You didn't . . . on both counts."

I didn't have many cards but I decided to play the strongest one, though it was still weak. Besides, if they intended to arrest me, we wouldn't be sitting in a police car having a chinwag. I'd be in handcuffs and headed to the Roundhouse.

"I didn't think the owner of the house was material to the case," I said. "The house is owned by a company and no one in the company was there at the time."

Turning even further to face me, O'Donnell said, "You expect us to believe that?"

I shifted in my seat because my side ached from my injury. But I didn't want them to know that. I'd have to work through the discomfort.

"I don't know what to expect you to believe," I said.

"I assume you've spoken to your brother-in-law about this. Where was Stuart Thomas on the night of the murder?" Thompson asked. "And remember, I can still arrest you for impeding a criminal investigation."

People passed by and casually looked in the car, noticing two white officers in the front seat questioning a Black guy in back. It was a racial stereotype that I hated and felt uncomfortable with, which is probably why I unconsciously scratched my forehead as if there was some itch.

"I can't answer that. I don't keep tabs on the guy," I said, waiting a heartbeat for a response from either of them that didn't come. So, I continued. "Listen, I know this man. He may be an ass but he's no killer."

"And this is based on what?" O'Donnell said, "Warm family moments during the holidays?"

This guy was really beginning to get on my nerves. But I couldn't let him rattle me. "No. It's based on knowing him closely for so many years."

"That's not enough. I have to bring him in for questioning. And what's he gonna tell me, Blaise?" Thompson said.

"I don't know. But please, keep this quiet for now, if you can. No one in the family knows anything about it and if Stuart's not involved . . . which I truly believe is the case . . . I don't want to upset things. It's why I've been working so hard," I said. "For my sister's sake . . . and their kids . . . please keep this quiet."

Thompson turned to face forward again, which was a signal to O'Donnell, who opened his door and got out. "I'll do what I can," Thompson said toward the front windshield. "We'll ask him to come in to answer some questions. We'll keep that quiet. It's all I can promise," he said, turning back to me. "But if he's arrested later, she's gonna find out. There's nothing I can do about that."

As I got out, O'Donnell had a self-satisfied expression. He looked at me closely and got back into the car, which then drove off.

I went into the bar and found Randolph exactly where I expected. This time he saw me coming as I got to the bar stool next to him.

"Bart, another drink for me and make it a double for my friend here. He looks like he needs it," Randolph said. To me, he said, "How ya doin', kid?"

"I'm fine. Just had a chat with the police that didn't go well."

"Yeah. I saw from the window. Thought you were a goner," he said. "But they didn't arrest you, so it could be worse."

"Yep, it could be worse," I said wearily.

The bartender refilled Randolph's glass after setting down a glass for me, which he filled with a brown liquid. "Here's to solving crime," Randolph said, clicking his glass to mine. He drank his straight down.

The brown fluid burned my throat, nearly causing my eyes to pop out of my head. I couldn't imagine how he kept downing this stuff day after day, year after year, and didn't destroy his innards.

"I need something." My voice barely sounded like my own, thanks to what I just drank. "I need some background on Organized Crime in South Philly."

"I expected as much. I thought you'd be out of your depth at some point," he said.

I coughed a little to clear my throat. "Before I get to that, update me on what you've learned regarding my friend's pregnant girlfriend"

Randolph glanced at his watch and then downed his last drink. He didn't address my comment, which I found curious, though I didn't mention it. "I know some about the Mafia but I have an expert for you. Let's get a booth," he said.

We got up and headed over to a booth along the wall that also had a good view of the front door of the tavern. I knew that whatever he was going to say, it was going to take a while.

CHAPTER XVIII

I had a theory that needed testing.

The wall was covered with War Bond posters from World War Two, interspersed with ad posters for long-dead beer brands. But it was a dark place, as if secrets were about to be shared, and smelled like the inside of an old ashtray, so Randolph probably felt right at home.

From some hiding place in his coat, Randolph pulled out a pack of unfiltered cigarettes. He pumped the pack upside down until a couple cigarettes peeked out of its opening. Extracting one, Randolph put the pack on the table and lit the cigarette.

He had been drinking for a while, I assumed, but his hands were as steady as mine. A blue haze of cigarette smoke rose over the table as he exhaled.

God, I hated smokers.

"Blaise, we discussed this. Remember?" he said. Randolph held the cigarette between the first two yellowed fingers of his right hand, which he moved around as he talked for emphasis. "I got you information on the doctor . . . where she practiced and what type of practice . . . and I told you it might be illegal to get more private info, and that it would cost you."

He looked at his watch again, then took a deep draw on the cigarette. I just sat and waited for the smoke. "And you said, hold off. Remember? That's exactly what you told me at the time."

I was about to say something, though the thought had yet to form in my head, when Randolph appeared distracted. The front door of the bar had opened and he was looking over my shoulder to see who it was. As I turned around to see for myself, Randolph raised his cigarette hand to beckon someone over.

"Georgie, over here," he said.

A middled-aged white man, wearing a gray overcoat that matched the color of his receding gray hair, walked in our direction. Randolph scooted over in his seat to make room for the guy, who sat down.

"Blaise, this is Georgios Aristidis, the best investigative reporter in the city and the most knowledgeable man around regarding the Mafia," Randolph said. "Works up at that rag on North Broad Street. Knows all the wise guys, and all the cops and the FBI."

He was also the most average-looking white guy I had ever seen, except for his piercing, inquisitive eyes behind metal-frame glasses. The guy reached over the table and a hand extended beyond the sleeve of his overcoat. I took the hand, which was fleshy and soft, yet held a steel-like grip.

"David Blaise," I said and looked quickly to Randolph for answers as to why this guy had joined us.

"Georgios Aristides. But everyone calls me Georgie," he said with an accepting smile.

"I asked Georgie to join us because he knows all the history and all the players better than me," Randolph said. "He can fill you in better on the Italian Mafia than I can."

"You exaggerate," Georgie said. "There's no one in the city with more sources than you."

"And you, my friend, are too modest," Randolph replied. To me he added, "This fella knows so much, one of those Mafia guys put a hit out on him."

Addressing Georgie, Randolph asked, "Whadda you gonna have?"

"I'm working. I can't drink now," he said.

"Wimp," Randolph replied and raised his hand to get the attention of the bartender. "Bart, a soda water over here and another round for me."

"Randy tells me you're a P-I . . . and a smart one. You're lookin' into Henry Cummings' murder and you want some information on Organized Crime. What do you need to know?"

"How did this Mafia war get started . . . between Patrese and DelMarco?" I asked.

"Angelo Bruno controlled everything here in Philadelphia and South Jersey for decades. He was into the normal stuff . . . illegal gambling, loan sharking, extortion, prostitution, some drugs but not much," Georgie said.

"He didn't care much for drugs, I heard," Randolph said. "Thought they were a plague. He was right about that, of course."

Georgie continued his story as the bartender brought over a shot of whiskey, and a glass and a bottle of soda water, setting it all on the table without saying a word.

"Some of the younger members of the organization thought Bruno's thinking was old-fashioned and they wanted to get more heavily into drug trafficking. They saw it as a huge cash generator. Bruno saw the potential but knew the downside," Georgie said, opening the bottle and pouring the drink into his glass. "It would dramatically increase law enforcement and scrutiny of the mob's activities, something Bruno wanted to avoid."

Randolph had started going through a bowl of peanuts, grabbing a load in his free hand, and throwing his head back and dropping them in a couple at a time. I sat quietly and nursed my drink. At least the drink took my mind off my aching side.

"Killing Bruno would take the consent of The Commission, the five mob families that controlled New York and that had some oversight of the local mob here," Georgie said.

"It didn't stop Bruno from being gunned down," Randolph added, blowing out some smoke. I tried not to choke on the smoke that was beginning to blanket me.

"No, it didn't," Georgie said. "The man who killed Bruno was ultimately assassinated, and in the worst way, but with Angelo gone, everything was up for grabs. In time, the Patrese faction came to the fore, pushing drugs and violently eliminating his enemies and lavishly rewarding his friends. The DelMarco faction, which is the closest off-shoot of Bruno's organization, is trying to hold onto the old ways. He wants to limit Organized Crime's expansion territorially and in the types of crimes they're involved in. He . . . that is Michele DelMarco . . . only wants good publicity, if he gets any publicity at all," Georgie said. And he took a drink of soda water.

"It doesn't seem to be happening, with all the killings," I said. "They're getting lots of publicity, and it isn't good."

"That's true, and New York noticed," Randolph said before downing more peanuts.

"The bosses called both Patrese and DelMarco up to New York a while ago to salve hurt feelings and calm things down," Georgie said. "They wanted to halt the killings, which hurt the organization locally and up in New York. And for a while it worked. Things quieted down."

I leaned back in my seat and crossed my arms over my chest as I thought. "Things don't seem all that quiet to me. There've been very public hits on both factions in the last week. What changed things?"

"It wasn't Henry's murder. It started before that," Randolph said.

"I have no idea, but something happened, maybe six or seven months ago, more or less, and it's been nothing but killings ever since. I've asked around but I haven't been able to figure it out," Georgie said. "Everyone down in South Philly's been asking about the Cummings killing, and the local cops, too. The feds don't seem too interested but that will change if they decide there's a connection to the ongoing war between the two factions."

As I listened, I got a better picture of how things changed and, perhaps, why. I had a theory that needed testing, though I didn't mention it to my two reporter companions. If true, it would clarify a lot. I just needed the proof.

And I needed it fast. Time was ticking down for Stuart.

I had called Stuart's office before I sat down with Randolph to let him know the police could be on their way. But he wasn't back in his office yet from meeting me in the coffee shop. After I finished with Randolph, I called again, but was told he was in conference and couldn't be disturbed.

I reckoned I knew what the conference was about.

Regardless of my feelings toward Stuart Thomas, he was family. He deserved the consideration of me calling to give him a heads up. I didn't know if Thompson or O'Donnell had made the connection with Allison but she didn't deserve the same courtesy I gave Stuart. And she wouldn't get it.

I hadn't figured out her place in all this, but I knew I would.

I was tempted to stop by my office on North Broad, but that would require me driving past my real destination closer to downtown and then driving back. I didn't want to waste either the gas or the time.

I pulled into the service station at Caleb and Broad and walked up to the building. It looked like dirty little gas stations all over the country, except that it had more internal and external cameras than one would expect with an establishment that sold gas at the pump, and an assortment of cheap candy, soda, and snacks at a counter inside.

Someone monitoring the cameras could probably see the entire property, front and back — leaving nothing to chance.

An old guy was sitting behind a counter that nearly came up to my chest. His clothes, a pair of well-worn black corduroy pants and a faded white shirt, looked like he hadn't changed them in weeks, and he sported a day-old stubble of gray on his chin.

He greeted me with a nod, and I bought some candy and paid for five dollars of gas.

"I need to talk to Chuckie," I said.

"He ain't here, I don't think," he said. "You with the PO-leese?"

"Not hardly," I said. "I'm a private investigator. I talked to Chuckie earlier this week. I'll leave a number for him to call. I need to hear from him soon."

The old guy accepted the card with casual indifference. On the back I wrote asking Chuckie to call me as soon as possible.

I felt eyes were watching me as I walked back to the car. Turning left onto Broad was a chore because of a faulty traffic light but I made it and was back at my office in only minutes. I stopped first to see Centerton.

"Larry, I've made some progress on your case," I said, sitting down in a chair before him.

"What ya got?"

"Nothing positive yet, but I'll know soon," I said, getting up because I heard my telephone ringing in back. "Excuse me for a minute."

He dismissed me with a wave of his beefy hand, and I reached my telephone just before the fourth ring.

"David Blaise Investigations," I said, not sitting down at my small desk.

"I heard you wanted to see me," Chuckie said over the phone. I was glad he didn't identify himself. Even over the phone I could tell he was nervous. Must be a natural condition. He seemed that way earlier, too.

"I have a couple of questions that you could clear up for me. But I can't ask now, on the telephone. Can I meet you?"

"What you want?"

"Not on the phone," I repeated.

"I need a lift downtown. Can you pick me up?"

"Sure. I'll be there in 'bout ten minutes. Meet you outside."

As I was leaving, Centerton asked, "When we gonna to talk?"

"Soon," I said, opening the front door. "I think I'm onto something, but I need to verify it. When I do, I'll let you know." I stopped and looked back at him, "Believe me, we're going to nail the bastard stealing the money."

He smiled and I walked across the street to my car.

~*~

As it is in all states, it's illegal to operate a motor vehicle in the Commonwealth of Pennsylvania without a driver's license. But people do it anyway. It's also illegal to drive without proof of insurance. People do that, too. The result of those two requirements is an epidemic of hit-and-run accidents in Philadelphia and in other areas of the state where there are a high number of uninsured or unlicensed drivers who don't want to get questioned by the police.

As I approached Broad and Caleb, I heard sirens in the distance. First checking my mirrors to see if they were behind me, I came over a slight rise in the road and saw the flashers coming from the direction I was headed.

At the corner of Caleb, a crowd of people had gathered and were blocking traffic. I managed to pull over and stop just as the ambulance arrived in front of the crowd. More police cars arrived, with officers moving people back and directing traffic around the scene.

I had a pit in my stomach as I walked up and I hoped it wasn't what I expected. At the edge of the crowd I looked down and there, on the ground, was Chuckie, emergency workers attending to him. But from the angle of his arms and legs, and from the look of his open eyes, I knew they were too late.

"What happened here?" I asked the man next to me.

"Car come 'round the corner too fast, hit the guy and kept goin'," he said. "Nutter hit-n-run in the city. Mayor's gotta do sum'hing 'bout it."

"Yep, he does," I said. "You see it happen?"

"I saw it," said a nearby woman in a heavy coat with faux fur trim along the edge of the attached hood. The coat had seen better days. She came over. "You with da cops?"

"No, just wondering," I said. "Imma P-Eye."

"Oh, like on those cop shows on TV," she said.

"Something like that," I said, taking out the notebook I always carried. "What did you see?"

"So this car, ya see, was cummin' down Broad. . . ." she said, but I interrupted.

"From which direction?"

"From Center City. So okay, this car was cummin' down Broad real fast like and he ran the light when he turned, he hit that skinny dude on da ground," she said. "The dude flew up in the air and came down hard over there."

"Did the car stop?" I asked.

"For a second. The guy stopped and got out. . . ."

"It was a man driving the car? How old was he? Can you describe him?"

"White dude's all I saw," she said. "That's 'bout it. He got back in the car and drove off."

I jotted down what she said. "You get a description of the car?"

"I don't knows cars, meself. It was maroon is all. But I saw the plate. Got sum of da number."

I was elated but didn't dare show it. "What was it? Pennsylvania, I assume."

"It was P-A plates. Numba was H-E-M one-seven-oh. I

kinda rememba cause that's my initials . . . H and M. Helen Matthews. I just have a way rememba-in' numbas. I come down to the gas station every day and play my lucky numbas."

I wanted to ask: *If they're so lucky, why do you keep playing them? Shouldn't you have won by now?*

I kept that to myself, however.

"Thanks Helen. Make sure you talk to the police officers over there," I said, and walked back to my car.

I hadn't talked to Clara for a couple of days — not since before my mugging — but on the drive home, I concluded the help I wanted was something only a law enforcement official could provide. Asking O'Donnell or Thompson was out of the question. And I knew Clara would still be at her desk.

"Clara, it's Dave," I said when she picked up the phone.

An angry silence hung in the air. I felt horrible about not calling her, but my reasons were genuine. My job required me to sometimes put my personal safety on the line, but I didn't want to worry Clara over issues that she couldn't control or do anything about. Perhaps that was selfish, but I needed to shoulder that burden alone, and to keep her safe.

But now, leaving the scene of the fatal car accident, I needed some answers and I didn't know where else to turn to get them.

There was a heavy exhale and a sigh on the phone before she spoke.

"What is it you want, David?" Her tone was so frosty she could probably chill a kettle of boiling water.

I got to the point. "I'd like for you to run a license plate number for me."

"Why should I?"

"Please, Clara. I really need this. Fast."

"You don't contact me for days and then, all of a sudden, you call me because you need something," she said. "What am I to make of that, David?"

I took a deep breath to give me a chance to think and to steel my resolve. I decided to lay some of it on the line. "I know we haven't talked and I'm sorry about it. I have reasons and I will tell you about them," I said. "Just not now. I promise I will. But I need this now. Please."

"This is the last thing I'll do for you until we have that talk you've been avoiding," she said, exasperation and acceptance in her voice. "Give me the damned number."

"Pennsylvania plates, H-E-M- one-seven-zero. Not sure of the make and model of the car, but I know it's maroon," I said.

"Give me a couple of minutes and I'll call you back. Where are you?"

"Home."

"I'll call you back."

I was in the kitchen pre-heating the oven to warm a TV dinner when the phone rang. It had only been five minutes and I didn't expect Clara to call back so soon. The SEPTA police department could tap into the state police database to get the information and she was authorized to do it. Still, this was faster than I thought I'd hear from her.

"David, where'd you get this number?"

"I saw a traffic accident on my way home from the office and thought I'd try to run down the number," I said, trying to sound innocent. Clearly something was up.

"The police have already flagged the tags and are looking for the car in a fatal hit-and-run. I may get a call from the police asking why I wanted to know this information."

"Whose car is it?"

"The plates belong to a car from South Philly registered to a Salvatore Ricci."

CHAPTER XIX

"The man was like a father to me. He was an angel, just like his name. A saint."

I noticed the lights were on as I walked up the five steps to the front door. I had a key, of course, but I wasn't sure of the reception I'd get, though judging from our last conversation I didn't think it would be great. So, I rang the doorbell and waited.

I always hated the sound of Clara's doorbell but didn't have a lot of time to contemplate it. Clara opened the door in only seconds.

"David?" she said, standing in the doorway, not budging.

"Can I come in? I want to talk."

She didn't say anything. But after a while, her lip on the left side went up in a sign of silent resignation and she stepped back. "Come on in. I couldn't stop you anyway. You've got a key."

While it was true — I had a key — it was not true that she couldn't stop me. But I didn't argue, at least not on that. I knew an argument was possible, indeed likely, but I didn't want it to start on something so trivial.

I entered and hung up my coat. Clara, not looking back, continued toward the back of the house. "I'm making dinner," she said.

Clara had a beautiful kitchen, which she renovated when she bought the house a few years earlier. What was once dark and foreboding was now bright and airy. The walls were white, and white IKEA cabinets lined two walls. But all the major appliances — refrigerator, stove, dish washer and microwave

— were all jet black, while the minor appliances — toaster, mixer, and canisters — were a fiery red. The diamond-shaped floor tiles were black and white.

The ceiling lighting was recessed and a large window over the sink bathed the room with natural light when it was sunny outside. There was a window box outside that was filled with flowers in the summer months.

She was chopping vegetables to lightly sauté in a pan. A pair of stuffed chicken breasts were already prepared to go into the oven. Clara had a glass of white wine — probably a Chardonnay — next to her, drinking a little as she worked. Her back was to me as she chopped at the counter next to the stove, where a pan with olive oil covering the bottom was warming.

"I really am sorry for everything, Clara. I didn't mean to hurt you."

"And yet you managed to do it anyway," she said while using a sharp knife to dice scallions.

I moved to her right side. Facing her and with my back to the counter where she was working, I said, "I want to show you something."

Clara stopped chopping and glanced down to my side as I lifted my shirt. "What the hell are you doing, David?" she said as I unbuttoned. Once it was fully open and she saw the bandage, her eyes went wide and she dropped the knife on the cutting board. "Oh my God, David, what happened to you?" Clara said, reaching out to run her finger along the edge of the bandage where it touched my skin.

There was a bright reddish-brown spot from where I had been bleeding since I last changed the bandage.

Looking back at me, she said, "What happened?"

"I survived."

"David!"

"You won't believe it if I told you," I said.

"Try me," she said. "Come over there and sit down." Clara turned off the stove then led me to a chair at the kitchen table. She took a chair and pulled it close, barely taking her eyes off my wound.

"I was attacked by a clown." I said.

"What?"

I was pleased with her reaction. "I was attacked by a knife-wielding clown outside my apartment building. Police think it was a mugging."

I knew that wasn't true but hoped it would pacify her.

"When?"

I wasn't looking forward to her reaction to the answer to that question. "Two nights ago."

"What? Two nights ago?" she said, getting up and looking down at me. The fear in her eyes regarding my safety was replaced with anger. She turned her back to me as if to walk away then turned to face me again. "And you're just now gettin' around to tellin' me this."

"I didn't want to worry you. You have a lot on your mind at work and I didn't want to burden you."

"So you say nothing. Is that it? You don't call me. You don't even have your grandmother call me. How could you?" she said. Her hands went to her hips and she was shaking her head in disbelief. "And I always thought Grammy Taylor liked me."

I looked away. And when I did, the realization must have hit Clara. She threw up her arms again and turned away once more.

"Oh my God! Oh my freakin' God, David. Don't tell me you didn't tell your grandmother, either," she said, looking back at me. "She'll kill you when she finds out. My lord, she'll kill me too, if she thought I knew and didn't call her. Who did you tell?"

Clara walked back to me and took her seat again.

"Valerie and Stuart. They came to the hospital and took me home."

"Stuart, too, huh? That's a surprise," Clara said with a huff.

I explained the incident in detail and that the weapon and the assailant were not found.

"Were you hurt badly?"

"Bad enough, but not as bad as it looks."

"It looks bad," she said.

"Mostly lots of blood. I'm getting good at changing the dressing without help."

"I wish you had told me, David. It's what hurts, that you withhold things from me, important things, like this," she said, reaching out toward the wound again without touching it. "I've always been there for you. You know that. But you keep holding me at arm's length."

"I'm sorry, Clara. I don't know what else to say. Or what else to do."

"Well, I know one thing you'd better do. Tell Grammy Taylor and make sure she knows it's not my fault for not calling her, because I would have," she said, getting up. "You well enough to help me with dinner?"

I cooked some rice as the chicken baked and then Clara sautéed some field greens, snow peas, red and yellow peppers, and onions.

I set the table — she always uses cloth napkins, saying it saves trees — and we ate and drank wine, mostly in silence. We were cleaning up and putting the dirty dishes in the dishwasher when I finally got up the courage to ask for something I needed.

"I think I'll go to Pittsburgh tomorrow to run down a lead on something. You have contacts there, right?" I said as I pre-washed the sauté pan in the sink before placing it in the dishwasher.

"Yes, a couple. What do you need?"

"I need help running down some names. You think someone there could help?" I said.

"If I ask," she said.

"Would you? It's very important."

"Whenever you ask me something you always say it's important," she said, taking the pan from me.

"It always is," I said, dunking another pan under the running water.

"You want this tonight? To call tonight?"

"If you can, yes."

Clara hung up her dish towel and headed for the dining room and then upstairs. "Are you staying the night?"

"I'd like to," I said, coming up behind her.

"I'll be gentle then, since you're hurt," she smiled and walked upstairs.

~*~

Pittsburgh is 300 miles away on the other side of the state from Philadelphia. The cities couldn't be more dissimilar. Pittsburgh is an industrial town dominated by two industries — steel, which was in decline, and coal, necessary for making steel. The U.S. Steel Corp. was still headquartered there.

Philadelphia was never dominated by a single industry but was still considered an industrial city, and, like most industrial American cities, was also in decline as the economic base in the country shifted away from hard industries.

Though different, both cities were linked by a single highway — Interstate 76. I-76 starts as the Schuylkill Expressway at the Delaware River over from New Jersey, and continues more than 300 miles as the Pennsylvania Turnpike across the state to Pittsburgh.

Clara made the arrangements at night before we went to bed. And I barely remember her kissing me on the lips when she headed out to work early in the morning. I knew she kissed me because once I was up and in the bathroom, I looked in the mirror and saw the evidence — a lopsided smear of lipstick from her kiss on my lips.

Before I got in the shower, I made a couple of calls myself, including one call to Raymond, who didn't answer. I selected something nice to wear, to be presentable to my Pittsburgh hosts, and headed out the door at a quarter to nine. I wanted to be in Pittsburgh by three o'clock but, after topping off my tank at the gas station around the corner, I still had a stop to make.

I drove west on Poplar for five blocks to the end, which faced Lemon Hill, one of the oldest parts of Fairmount Park. I took a quick left and then a right onto Lemon Hill proper and parked near a baseball diamond promptly at nine. I got out and walked over to some bleachers facing the field. Five minutes later, a clean, new Buick sedan pulled into the lot and Michele DelMarco, my new friend, got out and walked over.

He was alone, his compatriot having been blown up on his porch only two nights before. We were in the wide open and could see and react if anyone approached from any direction. But it offered zero protection against a shot from a high-powered rifle fired from a distance.

I doubted that would happen. Mob hits tended to be up close and personal. Besides, the wide open was the best security I could think of on the fly. I was glad he accepted it.

"Thank you for coming," I said.

"David, you said it was urgent and important. I respond to that when my friends call," he said.

"By the way, let me offer my sincere condolences on the death of your friend," I said.

"Thank you for your sympathy. There *will* be a payment for this, let me assure you," he said, and I was sure he meant it. But I didn't have a lot of time. I needed to get on the road and couldn't waste time with threats, even if they weren't directed at me.

"Mr. DelMarco. . . ."

"Mikie. We've been over all this," he corrected.

"Mikie, I was going to meet someone yesterday who I hoped would fill me in on some of the details of illegal gambling in North Philadelphia, but he was tragically killed last night in a hit-and-run accident," I said.

"Now you have my condolences," he said.

"I was hoping you might help me out now," I said.

"I don't know much about gambling in the north. Except for the Great Northeast, we don't operate up in North Philly."

"I see," I said, and forged ahead with a slightly different topic. "You were close to the late Angelo Bruno, weren't you?"

"The man was like a father to me. He was an angel, just like his name. A saint."

"Yes, well, okay," I said. What I thought was that Bruno was a violent, murderous patriarch, who hurt people merely for profit. But I wasn't about to say that. "Bruno's death and who will head the organization is at the core of your disagreement with Benito Patrese."

"Patrese is a schmuck."

"Yes, well, I get that too," I said.

"He wants to abandon all the old ways and expand the business in ways it shouldn't go," Mikie said, almost ignoring me.

"Tell me about the street tax."

"It's collected from anyone active in the areas where we're operating. We don't want to manage or control the activity in that area, such as slot machines or prostitution. But we provide protection and muscle, where necessary," he said calmly as if discussing the weather or the daily changes in the stock market. "It's divided amongst the various associates supporting the organization."

"How often is the street tax paid?"

"Angelo only required it once a year. But since the schmuck has been running things, he's sent his men to collect it monthly. And then sent muscle if it wasn't paid on time. It's a disgrace."

"Why?"

"Things were running smoothly before. Now there's chaos. Lots of blood spilt. This hurts the organization."

"Where did Henry Cummings come into the picture?" I asked.

"Angelo left all those people up in North Philadelphia alone. He didn't know the area that well and didn't need the headaches. They would pay a tax, but we stayed out of there," Mikie said. "I told Patrese to leave it alone, but he went to Cummings and demanded a cut of the action. Cummings refused."

In an excess of caution, I looked around the open field, checking again to make sure we were alone. After all, people were trying to kill Michele DelMarco, but he seemed totally relaxed as we talked.

"Patrese wanted to hit Cummings, but I insisted we take it to The Commission. They refused to okay the hit."

"Huh. Then his murder wasn't sanctioned?" I asked.

"No. That's why I'm trying to find who's responsible for it," he said. "It's why I came to you."

I paused in thought, though not for long, as I mentally considered, again, whether to say what I planned to say next. "You're being played," I said, almost casually

He stood up and faced me. "What?"

"By killing Cummings in South Philadelphia, someone is manipulating you and Patrese, pitting you against each other, perhaps hoping you two will eliminate each other," I said.

"How do you know this?"

"It makes sense. All the evidence points to it," I said. "But you're so busy trying to hit Patrese where it hurts or trying to protect yourself and your interests, you haven't noticed you're being manipulated."

"By who?"

I didn't have the nerve to correct him on grammar usage. "I don't know, but it's what I'm trying to find out."

"I'm also going to look into this. If what you say is correct, someone's going to get whacked. Nobody makes a patsy out of me."

~*~

I took the Schuylkill up past King of Prussia and got on the Turnpike, heading west toward Pittsburgh. I stayed on the Turnpike into Pittsburgh until I reached Forbes Avenue, where the Allegheny County Health Department is located.

Just before I arrived at my destination in mid-afternoon, I pulled over to call my contact, Joyce Shaw, a health department official Clara had known since college.

"Thanks for meeting me, Miss Shaw," I said once we met in the lobby of the building.

"Oh, it's no problem at all," she said, shaking my out-stretched hand. "And just call me Joyce."

"Okay, Joyce, where to?"

"The records department is upstairs. It's this way."

I followed her to an elevator and took it to the eighth floor. The elevator doors opened into a massive room with more file cabinets than I had ever seen in my entire life. "There's a table down here. I'll take you to it."

We found a long conference table along the wall at one end of the room. Apparently, it was there for when someone needed to go through a mass of files. I sat down and, at first, she sat next to me.

"Now tell me again what you're looking for?"

I had a week-old copy of The Philadelphia Inquirer with me and flipped it open to a page where I had circled a few names in red. "I'd like you to check for the birth records for any of these people. Not sure of all the ages but I know some," I said. "And I'd also like to see if you have any record or can show any connection between any of these people and the person whose name I wrote on the border. I wrote the name in blue ink."

"I think I got it now. Let's get started," Joyce said.

We went through numerous birth and death records, and she made calls to cross-check names with other departments for an hour. Once we were done, I had a nearly complete record of Henry Cummings' family, at least the ones in Allegheny County — his parents, his siblings and their families, his wife, and his children. Cummings moved to Philadelphia when his children were young, so those records would be in Philadelphia.

But the Allegheny County records provided a wealth of information, the implications of which played in my mind for the entire five-and-a-half hour ride home to Philadelphia.

~*~

It was past bedtime for the twins, Cora and Cody, when I pulled up in front of Stuart and Valerie's house in Elkins Park. It was a large, two-story structure that was made of stones native to eastern Pennsylvania. They had a beautiful, manicured lawn, with mature trees in front and well-maintained bushes along the foundation. The tree branches were bare, of course, and standing there like skeletal sentries, waiting to blossom in the spring.

The front windows to the left of the double front door were dark. The room was their formal dining room. The large windows to the right of the door displayed a grand piano, and there were lights on further back behind it.

Normally, Valerie turned in soon after the kids. However, lights meant Stuart was still up. I lightly rapped on the door, hoping not to wake anyone already in bed.

Stuart looked out a window and saw me. I heard the locks click and the door opened seconds later.

"Davey, what are you doing here so late?" Concern showed in his body language.

I whispered in case Valerie was still up. "Can we talk alone?"

Stuart looked back over his shoulder and back at me. "Everyone's asleep. Come in." Once I was inside, he softly said, "Is this about you know what?" I nodded and he took the cue. "We'd better go downstairs to the basement."

The basement was completely carpeted in a durable light tan, which felt great, even with shoes on. It was like walking on a tan cloud. To the right of the stairs was a home theater, with a large, pull-down screen and a projector for movies. Chairs were placed around the room for easy viewing and in the back of the room was an old-fashioned popcorn stand for making popcorn.

The room to the left in the basement was the adult room. There was a billiard table and a fully stocked bar. Four tall wooden chairs faced the bar and I got on one, while Stuart walked around to the other side and got two glasses.

"What'll you have?" he asked.

"Something light."

"I got soda and I got beer back here."

"A beer. It's been quite a day."

Stuart removed the glasses and pulled out two long-neck Budweiser's. We clicked necks and threw some back. Foam rose to the mouth of both bottles once we sat them down.

"The police came by the office yesterday and questioned me about the Catharine Street house and the shooting. I didn't say anything until my lawyer got there but we talked for nearly two hours," he said.

"What did you tell them?"

"The truth, which I'm not sure they believed. I don't know how Henry Cummings got in the house, or who killed him."

"They talk to Allison yet?" I said.

"I don't think they made the connection, but my lawyer thinks they will. He says I should be prepared for it, though it may take a few days," he said. "I don't know what I'm going to tell Valerie. She's going to kill me."

"She should." I looked toward the stairs to the first floor. "You're stupid for letting your dick get you into this situation." He took the admonishment without comment. Despite this current situation, Stuart was a smart man. He had probably already reached that conclusion.

I looked again toward the stairs before facing Stuart once more. "Don't be stupid again. Don't tell her anything yet. You say it could be a couple of days. I've almost figured this out. I can wrap it up . . . in a few days."

Stuart looked tired and harried when I arrived and now, he looked like a weight was lifted. I took the beer in hand but didn't drink any.

"What is it? Can you tell me?" he asked.

"Not yet. I don't have all my ducks in a row, but I'm getting there," I said. "Just try to stay calm."

I went into my jacket pocket and removed a list of names. "You can do one more thing for the cause. Tell my sister I stopped by after she went to bed but I need her to check the bank records for these people."

I handed him the list.

"You kidding me?" he said. "This name, too?"

"I'm not kidding. Have her check. Tell her some of their stuff may be hidden, so look hard," I said.

"I owe you for this. How much are you charging me?"

"You should have asked that at the beginning," I said. "But since you didn't, don't worry. I don't want your money. But you can do something for me."

"What is it? Anything."

"I want a new office. In a different part of town."

He glanced around the room as if it would provide the answer, and then smiled. "I got just the property for you.

Picked it up last year. It's in West Philly, on south Fifty-second Street, so it's near your apartment and away from . . . the family. Valerie, your brothers. They never go to West Philly. You'd think it was on the other side of the world. I just finished renovating it. Office space is ready for rental."

"Sounds promising," I said.

"I tell you what. You resolve this for me . . . and keep it away from me . . . and I'll let you have a corner office with two rooms . . . an outer office and an inner office. Looks out over the street."

"What's the catch?"

"There's no catch," he said.

"How much, then?"

"I can't let it go for free. It would look bad for business. You're my brother-in-law, for goodness sake," he said, starting to play hardball with the deal.

"Stuart, I'm saving your nuts here, not to mention your family."

"A dollar a month."

"For how long?"

"In perpetuity. For as long as I own the building."

"Deal."

"Deal," he said.

We shook hands across the bar.

CHAPTER XX

"The same thought has crossed my mind."

I felt good to get home. Things were finally coming together nicely. I wasn't at the end yet, but I could feel it coming. The trip to Pittsburgh hadn't been a waste. I found the names — and more importantly, the connections — of some of the conspirators in the Allegheny County records.

I dropped my keys in a bowl beside the door as I entered and called Clara on the telephone. I knew she was expecting the call without her having said so. I also didn't want a replay of the confrontation we had earlier.

"Was Joyce helpful? Did you find out what you wanted to know?" she asked.

"That and then some. It was a very good trip. Thanks for all your help."

"I was glad to do it."

"Look, Clara, I just got in and I'm exhausted. I haven't even taken my coat off. I wanted to let you know I'm home safely and to say good night," I said.

"That's good, Boo. I appreciate it. Have a good night. I'll call you tomorrow."

I hung up the coat and went to the kitchen for a soda. Back in the living room, I plopped down on the couch, Coke in hand, and watched the last of the eleven o'clock news and then Johnny Carson on The Tonight Show. I was so relaxed, I nodded off in the dark, only waking when I felt the soft drink can spilling onto my pants and on the couch. I got a towel from the kitchen to clean up the drink and sat back on the couch, intending to finish watching the show before getting to bed.

My eyes snapped open once my ears registered a ringing sound, although I couldn't tell what it was. I stared at the ceiling and was surprised at how light it was. In fact, the entire room was no longer dark. Light from outside was flooding into the room from the windows.

Without knowing why, I reached over to my right to pick up the telephone. The Today Show was on the television in front of me.

"Hello." My throat was dry and I barely got the words out.

"David, David. Someone's broken into my car."

My mind immediately snapped into focus. "Clara, are you all right? Are you hurt?"

"I'm okay. It happened overnight," Clara said, although she sounded shaken. "I called our department and the city police once I saw it. But I think you'd better get over here, too."

"I'll be right over," I said, hanging up and going for my coat.

The clock in my car showed it was after seven. From my apartment, it took nearly twenty minutes to get to her neighborhood. Parking was tight at that time in the morning, and I only found a parking spot about a block from Clara's.

Clara's car, a 1982 Honda Accord two-door coupe, was parked directly in front of her house. She was standing beside it, talking to a SEPTA police officer and a city policeman when I approached. The driver's side window was broken and shards of glass on the pavement reflected the morning light. It didn't initially look like there was any other damage. Smash-and-grabs were common in the area, generally going underreported because the damage was more a nuisance than a solvable crime.

Clara rushed over to hug me; then, taking my hand, brought me over to look more closely at the damage. "They haven't checked for fingerprints or anything," she said as she directed my attention to the inside of the car.

There was glass all over the driver's seat. But on top of that was a black-and-white photograph. Taken yesterday and from a distance, it was a picture of me sitting on the bleachers with Michele DelMarco. There was a note beside it that read: *Choose better friends if you don't want to get hurt.*

"What does it mean, David? Who did this?"

I was genuinely frightened for the first time, not so much for myself but for Clara. I hugged her tightly and continued to keep her close as I talked to the police.

"I don't know who did it but it's probably just some prank. Don't worry about it," I told her. But I instructed the SETPA police officer to take Clara to work and stay close to her when he did.

"I'll vacuum the glass out of the car and take it to an auto glass shop and have the window replaced," I said to Clara. "It'll take less than an hour and maybe a couple hundred bucks. You go to work. I'll take care of it."

When she left, I turned to the city police officer and said, "I need to talk to John Thompson. He works out of South Detectives. And I want him to see the photos of the car."

The officer reached inside the car and carefully took the photo and the note. I brushed the glass off the seat, got in and started the car, only thinking afterwards that more danger could be lurking beneath the car, such as explosives.

These guys do play rough.

But nothing happened, and I drove the car to Scott's Autoglass on Wilson Avenue in Southwest Philly. I was the fourth car in line that morning seeking a window replacement. Like I said, smash-and-grabs are common in Philadelphia, and Scott's was always busy early in the day.

By the time I got her car back home and parked, it was after eleven o'clock.

I went past my office to check on things and called Thompson from there. "I want to come down and talk. Did you see the photograph?"

"You mean the one recovered from the inside of your girlfriend's car? Yeah, I have it. But the question is, why were you meeting with DelMarco?" Thompson said.

"I can be down there in twenty minutes. Will you be there?"

"I'll be here waiting for you."

~*~

Thompson and his partner, O'Donnell, were sitting at facing desks when I arrived at the station. O'Donnell was on the phone and Thompson was typing. Both stopped as I came up.

"You must be getting close to something, Blaise, or is it that you just piss people off?" O'Donnell said.

"This is serious. These guys are threatening my family," I said.

"You got married?" O'Donnell said. Thompson visited him with a stern expression that the younger man ignored.

"You understand what I mean. You guys have got to do something."

The photograph was visible, sitting on Thompson's desk. He picked it up to study it. "Like what?"

"Arrest someone," I pleaded.

"Who? And on what charges?" Thompson calmly asked. "All we have is a picture taken of you and a mobster."

"We did tell you to not get involved in our investigation," O'Donnell said. "Maybe we should arrest you. You would be safe in jail."

I was tempted to say something but didn't.

"This was taken out in the open, as far as I can see. Anyone could have taken it." That was Thompson again.

I sat down closer to Thompson. "I need some help here."

"Johnny, would you get us some coffee, please? You know how I take mine. Thanks," Thompson said. O'Donnell took the hint, got up and left. Neither officer asked me if I wanted anything.

"I understand your predicament. But our hands are tied. You were meeting with a reputed mobster at a time when there's a major struggle going on in Organized Crime. But you were just talking, not committing a crime. No offense there, Johnny's comment to the contrary." He paused before changing the subject. "We're still looking into who attacked you. No weapon yet and, sorry to say, no leads, either. O'Donnell checked but there aren't any similar cases reported," Thompson said.

I felt my shoulder sag and, for the first time in a while, my side hurt. I felt helpless. It must have showed.

"I'll tell you what I'll do. We'll try to keep an extra eye on things . . . up near your girlfriend's way. There's a lot going on in this city that doesn't involve you. Corruption, racketeering, Organized Crime. And that's just today. But we'll do the best we can. Do you know anything that could help in our investigation?"

I leaned forward. "You could arrest Big Sally Ricci."

Thompson appeared shocked. "On what charges? Because someone broke the window of your girlfriend's car?"

"No, hit-and-run. That accident up at Broad and Caleb. The car was registered to Ricci. You know that."

"And how do you know that?" he said, sitting leaning forward in his seat. He stared at me intensely, waiting for an answer that wasn't coming. Then he sat back again. "Your girlfriend, Clara Perry over at SEPTA security. That's how you got it. She found it for you."

"I don't know what you're talking about," I said. "But that hit-and-run up on Caleb, I was at the scene just after it happened. I was coming to talk to him . . . Chuckie . . . the guy who was killed."

"About what?"

"I can't say."

"Blaise."

"Really, detective, I can't. Besides, he was killed before we had a chance to talk and I don't have anything important to share," I said. "What about Ricci's car?"

"It was an accident," O'Donnell said, returning with two coffees. He placed one at each of their desks. "But we don't know who was in the car. We certainly can't pin it on the owner, much as we might like."

"Ricci filed a stolen car report with the police two days before the accident," Thompson said. "We've canvassed the area for witnesses but it might just have been a hothead taking a joy ride in a stolen car."

"We can't pin that accident on Ricci. We can't prove anything and without that, we can't arrest anyone," O'Donnell said, leaning back and placing both hands behind his neck, a relaxed gesture though he looked anything but relaxed.

I started to get up and Thompson stopped me.

"Just so you know. We started a new Organized Crime Law Enforcement Task Force with the feds. There're so many killings, it's finally got the U.S. Attorney's attention. We're both working on it," Thompson said, indicating himself and his partner, "but O'Donnell is taking the lead on the task force from this office. If you find out anything, please make sure you mention it to him."

~*~

I was about to do something stupid. Moronic, really. But I felt helpless, and moronic was all I had left.

It was lunchtime. And I knew where Patrese would be at lunchtime.

On the corner of Bainbridge and 3rd was Marino's, a restaurant famed for its manicotti *and* for being a hangout for mob associates. Even the most casual observer of the Mafia knew from newspaper reports that Patrese ate lunch there every day, like clockwork.

I found a space on South Street and walked one block over.

The restaurant has a large picture window up front and a half dozen empty tables on the sidewalk for outdoor dining when weather permitted. Littering the walls were pictures of the owner, a man named Vito, with a host of local and national celebrities and entertainers. Each photograph was autographed by the celeb.

When I entered, Patrese was sitting alone at a table on the right side of the restaurant, near the wall but facing forward. A waitress, who was so shapeless you might not have known she was a female except that she wore a black skirt and white blouse, was carrying a tray of food to his table. Eyeing the approaching food, Patrese straightened in his chair and placed a white napkin in his lap. A bell over the door must have alerted him to my entrance because he looked up, as did a bodyguard who was standing to Patrese's right, and a second bodyguard, who was behind his boss.

Their attention momentarily wasn't on the waitress, who was placing the tray on the table with her left hand and raising her right. It wasn't empty.

I reacted instantly.

"She's gotta gun!"

What happened next occurred in a flash, although my mind recorded and dissected it in microseconds.

Just before the gun was leveled at the crime boss, the man to his right pushed Patrese out of the way and reached for his own weapon. Of the three bullets she fired, he caught two, with the third going wild. His falling body hit the table, scattering dishes and glasses but also obstructing the assassin's bead on her target, who was falling to the floor and slightly under the table.

The second bodyguard reacted slightly slower but more effectively, reaching into his shoulder holster and pulling out a .357 Magnum. It roared as he fired two shots, which lifted the assassin off her feet and threw her backwards, her arms flailing about and her weapon flying off. Blood expanded on her white blouse and started to pool on the floor under her.

Though violent, I was sure it was a merciful death. Given where she was hit, she would have died before hitting the ground.

The restaurant erupted in chaos, with people ducking under tables and behind the counter, which ran along the opposite wall. Patrese looked shaken but his bodyguard did not. With a cold, dispassionate expression that sent chills up my spine, he looked down at the dead woman, then pushed his severely wounded compatriot off the table where he had fallen. He extended a hand to help Patrese up.

"We got to get out of here," he said, pushing the crime boss toward the back of the restaurant. His gun raised and ready, he kept a watchful eye behind them as they headed for the back door.

"What kinda fool were you to come here? And what were you going to say if you got a chance to speak to him, assuming his boys didn't shoot you first?" Thompson asked me. We were standing outside, where a crowd had gathered. There were police barricades outside the restaurant. Onlookers were forced to stand on the other side of the street. Mob hits, successful or not, were scary but were also a spectator sport.

The area was flooded with law enforcement — local officers in blue and the feds with blue jackets with the letters FBI stenciled on the back.

I had already been questioned by the first officers on the scene.

"I was going to ask him to leave my girlfriend and my family alone," I said.

"But now he's going to think you put a hit out on him and came to see it done. Now we have to put a detail on you," O'Donnell said.

"What? Are you kidding me? I didn't put a hit on him. Why would I?"

"We know that, Blaise, but that's what Patrese is likely to think," Thompson said.

"What motive would I have?"

"That you're aligned with DelMarco," Thompson said.

I leaned against the building for some support. My head started to spin. Emergency medical personnel wheeled the seriously wounded bodyguard out of the restaurant and into the back of the ambulance.

Thompson looked down at his notebook and then up at me. "But I think we have a break, Blaise. We have an I-D on the shooter. She was one Maria Kovachev. Bulgarian. Wanted for a couple of hits in Europe."

"What in the world was she doing here?" I asked. "And who hired her?"

"Someone who wanted Patrese dead. Probably DelMarco," O'Donnell said.

"That makes no sense. He has his own hitmen for that. DelMarco would want to make sure the shooter could get close. He'd use local talent for that."

"Since you're so close to him, maybe you should ask him," O'Donnell said, tapping me on the chest and then walking back into the restaurant.

"What do you think?" I asked Thompson.

"I don't know," he said thoughtfully.

"I have a theory."

"Oh?" said Thompson. "Fill me in."

"This mob war . . . or at least the most recent part . . . is a distraction. Something else is going on," I said.

Thompson straightened his shoulders and looked hard at me. "Good observation, Blaise. The same thought crossed my mind."

~*~

I was back in my office doing paperwork later in the afternoon, work I detested. My small desk and the cramped space of my office was always cluttered. Stacks of papers, bills to file, invoices to complete littered most of the flat surfaces. I desperately needed clerical help but I had no place to put them, even if I could afford them. Once I took Stuart up on his offer to rent me office space in West Philly, I planned to get a secretary or an assistant, even if I had to starve myself to pay for them.

I heard the front office open and moments later Raymond walked into my office. Normally he was dressed to the nines — he was fastidious in dress, though a bit flamboyant — and today he was a surprise. He wore an old and somewhat faded Sixers jacket with a hood, a pair of gray sweatpants, and sneakers that had seen better days, which was saying something because to my knowledge, he didn't play basketball.

He had dark circles under his eyes, his hair hadn't seen a comb and a day's worth of stubble dotted his cheeks and chin. He looked like he hadn't slept in days.

Yet despite all that, he wore a smile that lit up my office.

"Man, it's been a long day and I don't have any updates yet," I started. "I tried you at home this morning and at your office this afternoon and couldn't reach you."

Though he sounded tired when he spoke, Raymond dismissed my comments. I quickly understood why.

"Audrey went into early labor last night and the baby — my daughter, our daughter — was born early this morning," he said with the largest smile I had seen on him since our school days.

"Ah, Ray, congratulations, man. That's wonderful news," I said, standing up to walk around my desk. We hugged like the old friends that we were.

Raymond started to pat his pants and jacket pockets as if searching for something. "Oh, yeah, I got a Polaroid picture of her here somewhere. Here it is."

He handed me a Polaroid snapshot of him in a battered gray sweatshirt that matched his sweatpants, with him holding a tiny baby wrapped in a blue and white receiving blanket and wearing a tiny pink cap on her head. Her eyes were closed, and she looked peaceful in sleep.

Raymond wore the pride on his face of a new dad.

"Raymond, man, I am so happy for you. Really. This is amazing," I said, handing him back the picture.

"She was early by several weeks. And just six pounds. But she's healthy. And so is Audrey. Both are doing well," he said. Looking at the picture, he added, "Isn't she the most beautiful baby you've ever seen?"

"Yes. Yes, she is. Just beautiful. Come over here," I said, making a place for him to sit down. "You look tired."

"I'm exhausted. I haven't slept since . . . I don't know when. Two days, I think. I was at Hahnemann all night last night."

"You guys pick a name yet?"

"She's named after our mothers. Mine and Audrey's," he said. "We named her Dorothy Grace."

Sleep deprivation and a weariness seemed to descend on Raymond's body, and he slumped back in his seat against the wall. And he looked at me with sorrow in his dark brown eyes.

"Davey, I'm so sorry for what I've put you through. And I will pay you, of course, but I'm sorry," he said.

I sat on my desk facing him. "For what?"

"I knew all along it was my baby."

I frowned. "Then why did you have me looking . . . from here to Mars . . . for information that doesn't exist? My options included doing something that was unethical and likely illegal. All to help you."

Raymond sat up as if a bolt of energy shot through his body. "Like what?"

"Never mind that," I said, wanting to avoid the true answer. "The question is still why?"

"I wanted . . . ah, I wanted," he repeated, searching for his thoughts, "To, uh, you know. Reconnect with you somehow."

I could see how hard it was for him to come up with the right words as he continued with me standing there. "We were close, back in school. It was fun. Sticking it to The Man by day and pleasing all the ladies at night. I missed that. That friendship. That closeness we had . . . before you joined the Navy and I headed to New Jersey for grad school."

I pulled over a chair and sat down. We were only a few feet apart.

"I didn't know how to get some of that back. As a result, I reached out to you in the only way I could think of. With a case," he said. "You must do all sorts of cases. Looking for criminals and the like. But this was all I had or could think of."

He waited. And I allowed a wry smile to appear on my face, easing the tension.

"Really?"

"Yes," was his reply.

I had a hard time expressing my feelings with a woman, other than with my sister or grandmother. But I imagined Raymond would accept a lot less than what a woman would be seeking.

"I missed you, too," was all I said. And was probably all that was needed to be said.

Reaching for some papers on the desk, I picked them up and needlessly straightened them before putting them back in their original place.

I should have been angry with him for sending me on a wild-goose chase. But I wasn't. His motives were good, even if his actions were not. And it was typical of Raymond, so self-centered, so dramatic. When he originally came to my apartment that night, all he needed was to say, "Let's get together and catch up." It's all he wanted and was enough for me. The made-up drama regarding his girlfriend was unnecessary, though not out of character for Raymond.

And at that moment, I didn't care. A newborn baby changes a lot of things. It certainly took my mind off my cases for a few moments — a few welcomed moments.

"It's no problem, Raymond," I said but changed the subject quickly to avoid any more manly embarrassment. "When can we see the baby? In person?"

"Soon, I hope. Doctors say since she's a preemie, she'll have to stay in the hospital a while longer. Several days. But she's doing well and she'll be home soon."

I ventured a tricky question. "Now that you have a baby, what about marriage?"

It was his time to smile. "One thing at a time, Snoop, one thing at a time." He got up. "What about you and Clara? Any marriage in your future?"

"Let me walk you to the door," I said, making the obvious diversion. "You look like crap. You should get home for a little rest. From what I've heard with a newborn, you're gonna need all the rest you can get."

Just as I reached the front door with Raymond, the phone on my desk rang.

"Excuse me, okay? I gotta get this. But I'll keep in touch. Promise," I said.

"You got it," he said. And after another quick manly hug, he left and I rushed back to answer the call.

"David Blaise Investigations."

"I think we've solved another Philadelphia crime, Blaise, although it's too late to get a conviction," Thompson said.

"Oh really? What? When?" I said, fearing the worst.

"From the shooting this afternoon," he said. "We found a car, a rental. It was under her name. Kovachev. Parked two blocks from the restaurant. She'd been working there for about three weeks." He stopped, apparently for effect. "And you know what else we found?"

"How would I know?" This was a stupid game, and I was tired. But he apparently was enjoying himself. I could almost hear him smiling on the other end of the line.

"In the trunk was heavy makeup, a tight, black jumpsuit and a bright yellow clown's wig. Plus, there was a map of the city. Your apartment building was circled," he said.

"You mean. . . ."

"It was probably a woman who tried to kill you, not a man."

My mind was in such tumult I hardly knew what to say. I felt slightly light-headed. "But I would have noticed. A woman?"

"It was dark and you said you were fighting for your life. Your attention would have been on the knife, not so much on the person holding it."

"I do remember he somehow felt strange when we were in close contact, but I just dismissed it. I was sure it was a man so that's what I saw."

"As I'm sure you already know, it's always best to keep yourself open to all possibilities during an investigation," he said.

"I will keep that in mind."

CHAPTER XXI

"Why would I come after youz? You're insignificant."

When he hung up, the telephone rang again, almost immediately.

"David Blaise Investigations."

"Did youz have a hand in any of this?"

I recognized the voice. "No, Mr. Patrese, I did not."

"Then it was that scum DelMarco. I'll kill 'im," he said.

"That may not be the case. There are other possibilities, Mr. Patrese."

"What youz sayin', hez not tryin' ta kill me?" Patrese said.

Shaking my head as if it would clear my thoughts, I said, "I don't know what I'm saying. I just know what I heard on the streets and in the papers earlier this year. You two called a truce and now you're at each other's throats again. Something started it. I don't know what."

"Why was youz in the restaurant today?"

"To ask you to leave my family and friends alone. Stop harassing me or them."

"I ain't harassing youz. What am I? Imma businessman. Why wouldz I come after youz? You're insignificant."

"Can I have that in writing?"

He laughed. The killer had a sense of humor. Who knew?

"I don't put nuthin' in writin'."

~*~

My phone was blowing up. The next call came from Valerie.

"Davey, I, uh. . . . No, never mind," she started.

"What is it, Val? You called me for a reason," I said before she had a chance to hang up. There was a pregnant pause on the line, followed by what sounded like sniffles, like she had been crying. Then I was really getting concerned. "Valerie, what is it? What's the matter?"

"I think I want to hire you to investigate. . . ."

Before she got another word out, I stopped her. "You're family, Val, and I don't have a lot of privacy in this office, as you know. Whatever it is, it's best not to do it over the phone. We should talk in person. I can come meet you."

"We can't talk here, either."

"Did you get the list I left with Stuart?"

She didn't say anything at first. And when she did, it sounded like she was about to cry.

"I have it. I found what you were looking for. And I checked with a friend over at PNB. They had some interesting stuff there, too. But we can't talk about it here, not in the office," she said.

"Can we walk and talk?" I asked.

"I've seen you do it before," she said, adding a little humor.

"Then whenever you're ready."

"Give me an hour to tidy up my desk and then I'll head out. I'll meet you at Reading Terminal."

~*~

Valerie and I were sitting in the booth at an Amish diner in the terminal market. Very pale, young, white women in plain pale blue dresses with white aprons worked behind the counter. It wasn't busy but they left us alone at first.

Once settled, I brought up the question that had been on my mind since before we hung up the phone. But Valerie apparently had sufficiently recovered emotionally that she quickly cut me off.

"You," I started hesitantly, "said you wanted me to investigate something. When we were on the phone."

She dismissed the comment with a casual wave of the hand. "It's nothing. Not important. Sorry I brought it up."

"You didn't bring up much. Or anything, really. But if I can help. . . ."

An awkward silence followed. And I realized Valerie was facing an uncomfortable truth, probably about her husband, but clearly wasn't ready to share it. I opened my mouth to say something, although I wasn't certain what would come out. Brotherly reassurance? Comfort? What do you say?

But I was saved from saying anything when a server finally arrived to take our order. I ordered cherry pie. Valerie only wanted coffee. Once we were alone again she took a document out of a folder and spread it out on the table, facing me.

"Is that what I think it is?" I asked.

"Yes, you got it right. He set up a dummy company that, on paper, owns your detective agency. You have four highly paid employees, including yourself. It's how he's accounting for the stolen money. He's laundering it through your agency. He even pays taxes on it."

"Won't that affect me, tax wise?"

"Yes, but the accounting firm does all your taxes, which is why you haven't noticed anything. You obviously didn't look closely when you signed your return," she said.

I considered my financial and tax position as I chewed on a slice of the pie. "Am I . . . in trouble with the IRS?"

"You'll need a good tax lawyer. I have one I can suggest. He's worked for the bank before and he's good," she said. "And, he's Black." Valerie blew on her coffee before taking another sip. "You'll need to file amended returns for the last, let me see here. . . ." She put down the cup and turned the paperwork around to see it better, then turned it back to me. "You'll need to refile for the last two years."

"How much money was he stealing?"

"I'm not sure because I can't tell how long he's been doing it. He may be using other shell companies involving other clients," she said. "It's up to a forensic accountant to figure all that out."

I cut a sliver of pie with a couple of cherries on it and put it in my mouth. The pie was excellent, the filling sweet and delicious, the crust light and flaky. After I swallowed, I moved the conversation along.

"What about the others?"

Valerie stacked the documents on top of each other and pushed the stack over to the side. Reaching down, she took out another bunch of papers, plus a manila envelope.

"Look here," she said, pointing to two sets of some papers on the table. "This is a trail of money from my bank to a bank in Switzerland, and then back to a branch of Philadelphia National Bank. I have a friend there who owed me a favor and got me this information. Together with the records from PSFS, we have a clear trail of money laundering. This person should go to jail."

"They probably will, once I show police this information," I said.

"They can't know how you got it. I'd be in big trouble. My friend would be, too."

"Don't worry. I got your back."

I packed the papers up and was placing them in the envelope when Valerie reached across the table and took my hand.

"I'm worried about Stuart. He's been very tense for the last couple of weeks," she said. "And you talked to him alone in the basement of Grammy Taylor's house a couple of weeks ago, and you stopped by the house late last night. You thought I was asleep but I know you two went into the basement. What did you talk about?"

I tried not to look nervous. "It was nothing. Sports, mostly. And I needed a little manly advice on women . . . well, Clara . . . and I reached out to him."

She looked like she didn't believe me and I could see why. It was lame. But it was all I had on the spur of the moment.

"You wouldn't lie to me, would you, Davey? Don't lie to me."

I felt like I'd been stabbed again and it hurt. One day she'd most likely find out about her husband's affair if she didn't already know. But it wouldn't come from me. And it wouldn't be today.

"Just man talk, Val," I said, thanking her again for the help on the case.

I was about to get up to leave when she grabbed my arm. "I'm worried about you, too, Davey. And it's been a while."

"Are you talking about Clara again?" I asked.

"No, it's not just that." She looked down at the table as if to consider how to approach another subject. "You spent all that time a couple of years ago at Temple taking law school classes at night. Why'd you stop? You always said you wanted your law degree. What changed your mind?"

This was a touchy subject, which was why I rarely discussed it.

"Valerie," I started, and stopped. "Val, I just ran out of money. I'm barely hangin' on now."

"David, I know that's not the only reason. There are other resources to help. You know that."

I didn't want to continue but, for some reason, felt I owed her something. "And, well, my time has past. I'm getting too old for it. School."

"Don't be ridiculous, David," she retorted sharply. "You're what this year? Thirty-two? You're young. You've got time. You just have to do it."

"And there's . . . Temple."

"Yes, I get it. You always wanted to go to Penn for a law degree. The prestige," she said. "How many credits do you have?"

"About half what I'd need to graduate."

"Listen, I have a friend at Penn law school," she said, and I started to object but she stopped me. "No, listen. She was a professor of mine in financial ethics class at Temple but she's now an assistant dean at Penn law school. I talked to her about you and she said there's financial help you can get and that the law school could accept most, if not all, of your Temple credits. There are night and weekend courses you could take, though some of the time you'd have to attend full-time. But it's doable, David. You should think about it. It's what you've always wanted since before I can remember."

Valerie was right about that, though in recent years I hadn't said much about it to her, or to anyone in the family.

"Okay, Val. I'll think about it," I said, more cheerfully than I felt. However, I cautioned her, lest she get either of our hopes up, "I can't do it this year. Maybe next year. In the fall. And only if I'm doing okay with the job. But let's keep this just between you and me. I don't want any pressure from Grammy, or anyone else."

"Deal," she said, and was about to get up when I stopped her. Remembering school, I suddenly had more to say.

"Oh, by the way," I said. "You remember my old high school-slash-college friend, Raymond, right?"

"Yeah, the cute one. I had such a crush on him when I was little."

"Well, it's too late now. His girlfriend just had a baby. A girl. Dorothy Grace," I said.

"Good for him," she said, excitedly.

My thought exactly.

CHAPTER XXII

"Don't worry. It's not loaded."

It had been a tiring couple of weeks but thanks to some help from Valerie, as well as my own investigative footwork, I thought things were coming to a conclusion. I felt a relief as I left my office and headed home at the end of the day.

On my home phone, I called Randolph but only reached an afterhours receptionist. I left my name but no message. I then called Georgie, knowing he had a much later deadline, but he had already departed for the day. The reporter who answered his phone said she'd leave my name and number, but I said I'd try again in the morning.

In the kitchen, I heated up a frozen TV dinner of what was supposed to be sliced turkey with mashed potatoes and gravy but it was so bland I was sure my taste buds would revolt if I ate more than half of it. Pushing it aside, I was left to sip a beer, long for some of Grammy Taylor's leftovers and consider my next steps in the morning.

Back in the living room, I pulled a manila envelope from my desk drawer and addressed it. Not sure how much the postage would be — it wasn't going far — I rummaged through my desk drawers until I found what I hoped would be enough leftover one- and two-cent stamps to cover the cost. It looked a mess on the outside, but it was the inside that mattered.

And getting it to the right people.

Walking out of my apartment building — and checking both directions as I did — I hurried down to the mailbox at the corner and deposited the envelope. As a precaution in the unlikely event there wasn't enough postage, the return address was the same as the sender. It would get there either way.

Mrs. Findley was in the hallway when I returned. She was a sweet, quiet woman and I think she would have preferred I had another occupation. Though they had never met, she and Grammy Taylor would probably get along quite nicely.

"I'm sorry, David, but I'm going to have to raise the rent on the apartment soon," she stammered in a timid voice. I got the impression she would rather die than continue the conversation. It was that painful to her. "My taxes are going up and I just can't afford it anymore. I need to raise the rent."

"Don't worry about it, Mrs. Findley. I love it here and the rent is more than reasonable," I said, then considered what she might be saying but didn't. "Are you saying you'd like for me to leave?"

The question so shocked her she stepped back toward her apartment, as if it provided her protection against such a blasphemous question. "No, no, no. I didn't mean that. I just need to pay my bills. The taxes are killing me."

"It's no problem, Mrs. Findley," I said, maintaining my distance, lest I scare her again. "How soon?"

"In two months. It says in your lease I must give you two months advance notice. But if you need more time, I can wait to raise it until later," she said. Turning to indicate inside her apartment, she continued, "I made you some cookies. Left them in a tin at your door just now. I knocked but there was no answer. Didn't know you went out."

"Two months is fine. Thanks for the notice and the cookies," I said and headed upstairs before I had to endure more apologetic conversation.

Mrs. Findley was an excellent cook and made extraordinary baked goods. Her cookies were a bonus to renting from her and I was deeply grateful for them after such an unsatisfying dinner.

The cookie tin was outside my door and the phone was ringing when I walked inside. I rushed to answer it.

"Hello."

"Is this David Blaise, the detective?" asked a female voice. It sounded familiar. "It's Allison Charles. I'm sorry to call you so late. I'm not bothering you, am I?"

"No, it's fine."

"What I was really wondering is whether we could talk . . . face-to-face."

I looked at a clock on my wall. It was nine-forty-five in the evening. "You mean tonight?"

"Yes. I have a very busy schedule tomorrow and there are some things I'd like to clear up as soon as possible," she said. "I tried to reach you earlier at your office."

"I must have been out but I didn't see that you left a message. I would have returned the call," I replied. "Where would you like to meet?"

She didn't answer the question directly but kept talking. "I didn't leave a message. I had a busy day in the office and so I waited until this evening to reach you at home. I hope that's okay," she said earnestly.

"I understand. It's okay. What can I do for you?"

"I wanted to explain some things but, well, I'm home now and would prefer not going out again. Would you mind terribly coming over here to my house to talk?"

I considered it for a moment. I didn't know what she had on her mind or what she was going to say but it would undoubtedly be interesting, and perhaps even true. And all I had planned for the evening was catching up on reading.

I asked for the address, although I already knew it. "I'll be there in fifteen minutes."

"I look forward to seeing you," she said.

I bet you do, I thought after I hung up the telephone.

I retrieved my weapon from the kitchen and headed out again.

Allison had a beautiful townhouse on a quiet street in a wealthy area near Fairmount Avenue, only a stone's throw from the Art Museum. I was sure it was great on the Fourth of July, because she could look out her window to see the city's annual fireworks display. The pyrotechnics were set off just behind the museum at the famous water works along the Schuylkill.

I noticed she had a short driveway in front, which was rare in this part of town. I could have used it, although her car was already there, but it would mean the tail of my car would block part of the sidewalk.

No matter. I found a parking space, although it was three blocks away.

I pushed the button for the doorbell and the door was almost immediately opened. She must have been standing by, ready for my arrival.

"Come in, won't you?" said Allison, still in a dark knee-length pencil skirt and blue silk blouse. She must not have been home long. She hadn't changed yet into comfortable clothes.

I entered a brightly lit hallway, with a living room to the right.

"This way," she said, leading me into her living room. "Have a seat."

This was the house of a single woman. No parent would want a small child in this room. It was clean and straight. The couch was an off-white cotton fabric with a matching loveseat.

I sat on the couch and she briefly sat on the loveseat.

"Oh, pardon my manners," she said, jumping up. "Would you like something to drink? Wine? Sparkling water? I might have some juice."

"No, thanks. I'm good," I said.

"I'll just get something for myself. Would you like some cheese?"

"I don't need anything. Thank you," I said.

She left the room, turning to the right and heading down a hallway. But she kept talking. "As I think about it, we got off to a rough start. I know you were just trying to do your job. Stuart told me he hired you. Not right away, though I wish he had. It would have made things easier."

"How so? Made things easier?" I asked.

"You don't mind if I have a glass of wine, do you?" she called out.

"No, go ahead."

Her heels echoed down the hallway as she returned. She had a half-filled glass of wine in her left hand and a gun in her gloved right hand. My heart skipped a beat. Because of the gun, not the wine.

She placed the gun on the table in front of me along with the glove after she took it off. Sitting back on the loveseat and crossing her legs, she could not have been more relaxed if she tried. She obviously felt she was in total control.

And she clearly felt I wasn't.

"We would have understood our roles better if I knew about you before our first encounter," she said. Allison drank her wine and studied my reactions. "Don't worry. It's not loaded."

"What are you trying to pull?" I said, though I tried to remain calm. I went from looking at the gun and then back to her. She only smiled.

"I'm not trying to pull anything. I'm just setting the record straight," she said. "But don't you recognize that gun? Surely you do."

This time she moved forward and set the wine on the table beside the gun, which she studied closely but didn't touch. Then she looked up at me.

"It's the gun that I used to kill my Uncle Henry. Never saw it coming. He liked me to choke him when I was on top and we were having nasty sex. He was unconscious by the time I got the gun from my purse beside the bed," she said.

I reacted apparently with some shock.

Allison frowned at me. "Now, don't pretend. You knew he was my uncle. You found that out when you went through my family's records in Pittsburgh. And, yes, I know about that, too."

It wasn't knowing that Henry Cummings was her uncle that caused the shock. It was the casual way she talked about an incestuous relationship and then killing her victim in his sleep. No anger at him for the relationship or remorse at killing him.

She sounded proud. And nuts.

"Charles was your maternal grandmother's maiden name," I said, contemplating whether to pull out my weapon. She wasn't making any threatening moves, so it didn't seem necessary now. But surely a moment would come when I would need it. After all, she just admitted committing a murder. And since everything she did was for calculated effect, that was planned, too.

"I took the name as a child because my grandmother raised me. Uncle Henry was on my father's side. I never took that name." She frowned at me again, apparently disappointed. "You don't recognize the gun?"

I looked closer but also didn't dare touch it. Then it dawned on me. I looked at her in awe. "It's Stuart's gun."

Allison clapped her hands together in obvious joy.

"That's right. Well done," she said. "It's what I'm going to use to frame your horny brother-in-law. Once the police find the gun tomorrow and run ballistics tests, they'll conclude it was used in a couple of killings."

"Killings?"

"Oh, yes. More than one. But let me get to that later. You must have loads of questions. It's why I asked you over. To answer them before it's too late. For you," she said.

"Why did you kill him?"

"Besides the fact that he was a sexually obsessed dinosaur living in the past? Because I wanted to make the city safer AND make some money doing it."

I considered what she might be getting at and Allison waited for me to do the mental exercise. As she waited, she got up, walked over to a table where there was a pack of cigarettes and took one, lighting it with a lighter on the table. She brought an ashtray with her when she returned to the loveseat, blowing blue smoke into the air.

Man, I hate smokers, I thought. But at that same moment, the answer struck me. "You're the new boss, the person now running his gambling operation. You're the silent partner."

"Precisely. One of them, at least. My partners and I thought it was best to consolidate some activities," she said, leaning forward to drop the cigarette in the ashtray and to take her glass again. She twirled it, watching the liquid curl around inside the glass. Then she took a sniff, closing her eyes and enjoying its full-flavored aroma. It was only then that she drank some.

The woman was insane.

"You see, people think I concentrated on urban economic development at Wharton. No, it was mergers and acquisitions. Good planning's a requirement for successful mergers or acquisitions. And that's what this is," she said, taking the cigarette once more and inhaling. "There's all this crime and violence throughout the city, which makes economic development more difficult. It's hard to interest investors in projects when there's all this crime, even when the crime couldn't possibly affect them. So, by consolidating some so-called criminal operations in north and south Philadelphia, and eliminating much of the competition, the streets will be safer and investments will grow in the city. It's a win-win for everyone."

"Not for everyone. Not for your victims," I argued.

She dismissed the thought. "Then they don't matter."

"You're consolidating with who?" I asked.

"It's whom," she corrected. "'You're consolidating with *whom?*'"

Damn Ivy League education. Almost made me reconsider taking classes at Penn law school. "With whom?" I said.

"Me." I didn't hear him coming, but Big Sally walked into the room and Allison stood up. He kissed her left cheek as she blew him a kiss, not getting any lipstick on his cheek or his clothes. He softly slapped her butt and came over to me. "Stand up."

He was menacing and I knew I didn't have a choice but to obey. He had kept his right hand in a jacket pocket, which probably held his gun.

He patted me down and took my gun, depositing it in his left jacket pocket. Then he sat on the couch at the other end from me.

They both were incredibly well-dressed. Were the circumstances different, I could imagine we were three Yuppies getting together for a drink and a few laughs. Any laughs tonight, however, would surely be at my expense.

"I read the situation. We both did," Big Sally said, looking at Allison, then back to me. "We needed to grow, to expand. I had to take charge. Move obstacles in my way."

"Henry didn't understand, either. He didn't believe me when I told him it was best to ally with some guys in South Philadelphia. It made strategic sense," she said. "Strategic planning was what he paid me for. It's why he paid for all my college education. But he just wouldn't listen."

"I suppose you didn't tell your uncle you were in debt, either," I said. "Didn't mention that."

Allison sat back further in her chair and appraised me closely. Her right arm was bent at the elbow and she held the burning cigarette away from her body. "Wow. That was nice.

You do have some good sources," she said. "Yes, I was in debt."

"To me," Big Sally said. "I oversee gambling operations. Numbers, slots, you name it. It's me."

"And you couldn't just go to your uncle and say you owed money to the mob and that they approached you. That they planned to muscle their way in if they had to. You kept that quiet and struck a deal with Patrese and his lot," I said.

"Not the boss. Just me," Big Sally said. "But first we had to deal with some obstacles in the way."

"And that would be Michele DelMarco and his people," I said.

"And my father-in-law, too. Benito the Baker," Big Sally said. "Didn't know *that*, did you, Mr. Know-It-All? A lot of people don't."

"Salvatore and his partner came to me with a proposal," Allison said. "We get Patrese and DelMarco duking it out. And if they didn't eliminate themselves on their own accord, we'd help them along."

"I guess that's where the Bulgarian assassin comes in," I said.

"You're catching on," he said.

"It had to be done," Allison said. "For everyone's good."

"Who's your partner?"

Big Sally and Allison glanced at each other. But it was Sally who answered. "My cousin Giovanni."

"Who killed Chuckie, up on Caleb and Broad a couple of nights ago?" I asked.

"One of my guys. We'd been waiting for the opportunity. When my guy saw the chance, he took it," Big Sally said. "I sent him to South Florida on the very next flight."

"You didn't know I was on my way to meet him? To talk," I said.

"No, we didn't find that out until later," Allison said and looked at her partner. "We were just lucky on that one."

"Chuckie. He wasn't," I said.

"Chuckie wasn't close enough to know about me. But he could cause trouble. He had to go. A casualty of war, as you will be also," she said. "You were just a nuisance . . . at first. A struggling detective with only one client on retainer, and virtually no active cases. It amazes me that you've survived for so long on so little."

"You having a change of mind about me? I'm more than just a nuisance?" I asked.

"Oh, yes," Allison said, although it looked like Big Sally didn't agree. "You proved to be resourceful and persistent. We can't have that."

"That's why you started threatening me," I said.

"Salvatore here sent his Bulgarian assassin first," she said, with an edge to her voice. It must have been a strategy they didn't agree on.

"We couldn't just have her shoot you from a distance with a sniper rifle. It would draw too much attention to your death," Big Sally said. "She suggested the knife attack, although it wasn't her first choice. But it was supposed to look like a simple mugging."

With eyes as cold as ice, Allison said to Big Sally, "And despite her assurances, she failed. And that failure brought a lot of attention . . . attention your untimely death, Mr. Blaise," she said, looking back at me, "was to avoid."

They didn't address each other for a while. And I began to wonder whether they had thought out the end game of their alliance. Allison was obviously willing to sleep with someone if it fit into her agenda — Stuart, her uncle, even Salvatore Ricci. And Big Sally couldn't have reached his lofty position in organized crime unless he was willing to spill someone else's blood. I wondered which of them would reach the inevitable conclusion that their agreement had run its course and that the other was expendable.

Who would try to kill who first? I thought, then corrected myself. *It's whom. Who would try to kill whom first?*

"Did Maria Kovaschev know that you planned to kill her after she assassinated Patrese in the restaurant?" I said.

"How'd you figure that?" Big Sally said.

"It makes sense. She was a loose end. You take care of loose ends," I said.

"Like you," he said in a menacing way.

"He's right, you know. You were supposed to be at the restaurant and were going to kill her to divert any suspicion from our little endeavor. But you were hung up in traffic coming back from Atlantic City and didn't get to the restaurant in time," Allison said, and then looked at me again. "I think it's cute that you figured that out."

"And you guys are going to stick to the story about the hit-and-run driver being sent to South Florida?" I said to her.

"My, my, my. You *are* good. How is it that you haven't been more successful?" she said. Allison's attention switched back to Big Sally. "Our partner said he took care of that loose end this morning."

"What partner?' I asked.

"Enough of this shit," Big Sally snapped, standing up and ignoring my question. "I've had enough. Time to end this."

Allison calmly got up and moved to his side, gently putting her hand to the nape of his neck and moved up close to whisper sensually into his ear, without taking her eyes off me.

The woman was still insane but I came to the quick conclusion that when the time came to end their relationship, she would be the one standing over Big Sally's corpse, not the other way around. And although he should, the mobster wouldn't see it coming — not until it was too late.

"Don't let him rattle you, Salvatore. We've come too far," she said. Pulling back a little, she continued, "And you know we can't kill him here. We agreed on that."

With her gentle, seductive touch on Big Sally's shoulder, I could almost see his dick harden.

"Get up, Smart Guy. We're leaving," he said, taking a hold on the gun in his pocket, and picking up the gun on the table with his gloved left hand.

Allison stepped back to allow us room to maneuver around the couch.

"Where to?" I asked.

Big Sally indicated where I should go with the gun he still hadn't removed from his pocket. "The car's outside."

Allison turned off the entry light in the ceiling before we reached the front door. No one would see our shadows from the outside. I was closest to the door and Allison stepped close to Big Sally.

"You'll be back tonight, baby?" she said.

"It'll be late. It'll take some time to do this right."

"I'll still be here waiting," Allison said, giving him a kiss on the lips. Big Sally used his free hand to grope her ass.

It was his way of showing me the prize he'd claim again after I was dead. Though I was in mortal danger and had yet to figure a way out, I thought, *"You two should go get a room."*

For some reason, I almost felt sorry for poor Salvatore "Big Sally" Ricci. He didn't appear to know that one day her kiss would be his Kiss of Death.

She turned to me. In the darkness, I noted a touch of sincerity in her voice. "I'm sorry it must be this way. I think you're cute."

She then kissed my cheek, turned the handle, and opened the door.

CHAPTER XXIII

"I hope you can swim."

I started down the steps with my executioner behind me, a hidden gun pointed at my back.

"To the left at the bottom and go to the corner and turn right," he said.

I did what he said without comment. But then I felt his left hand in my back just below my neck and he pushed me hard. I nearly tripped and fell.

"You think you're such a Smart Guy, so cute," he said as we continued walking. "She won't think you're so fuckin' cute once I blow your brains out." I slowed to say something and was turning around but he pushed me hard again. "Keep going and keep your fuckin' mouth shut."

I got to the corner where a tall apartment T-boned Allison's street. "To the right, over there behind the building."

I wanted to run but I knew it would be a fatal mistake. I didn't want to go behind a building in the dark of night with a gun pointed at my back, but I knew he'd shoot me if I deviated even slightly from his instructions.

As we approached the back of the building, I was surprised to see the maroon sedan wanted in the hit-and-run accident sitting there. I walked up to it, not knowing that Big Sally had stopped. When I turned around, I had to react quickly as a set of keys flew toward my face.

"Open the trunk. You gotta get somethin' out," he said.

You mean you're going to put me in it, I thought.

I inserted the key and turned the lock and the trunk popped

up. Another surprise. It was already occupied. Even in the poor light I could see the body of Benito "the Baker" Patrese, his eyes closed and a little red hole in his forehead.

Even in death, the man was impeccably dressed. His dark gray, double-breasted suit was buttoned and his pants still had a nice crease. The shirt was white with French cuffs. The white and gray tie had a nice pattern. He could be going out to an expensive affair, except that he was crammed into the trunk of a car. Given the odd position of the body, I assumed he was killed first and later stuffed into the cramped space.

A shovel lay across his body.

"You're gonna use that to dig his grave before I deal with you," Big Sally said, throwing the murder weapon into the trunk with the corpse. He finally had the other gun out for me to see. "Get the keys and close the trunk. You're going to come around here to the passenger side with me."

I closed the trunk as he backed away to allow me room to walk around the car. "It's unlocked. Open the door and slide in over to the other side, the driver's side," he said. "One wrong move and you're dead."

I was certain he meant it.

I got in and scooted over the gear shift lever and into the driver's seat. Big Sally got into the passenger seat beside me.

The car looked nice. But then, nearly every car newer than mine looked nice to me. Cloth seats, cup holders behind the gear shift, automatic, AM/FM radio with a cassette deck, power windows and door locks, even power for the sunroof.

Sweet.

"Start the car."

"Where are we going?" I asked.

"Don't worry about it. Just drive where I tell you. Now get going. Back us up slowly and head down the street to the next corner. You're going to East River Drive."

Philadelphia is full of narrow streets packed with cars with little space to maneuver. But the river drives, one on the west side of the Schuylkill River and this one, on the east side, were heavenly to drive, particularly when there was little traffic. Both were four-lane roads — two lanes in each direction, though at times the lanes narrowed as the road snaked along the river.

Stretching from the Art Museum to the base of the Lincoln Drive, East River Drive was four miles of straights and sometimes challenging curves. Traffic was always fast. Often there was no runoff to the right, and only the double-painted yellow lines on the street separated a driver from the on-coming cars to the left.

Beyond that, on the right of the in-bound traffic, was the river.

When I could, I loved speeding along the river drive in my Mustang, always taking each curve at the right speed to maximize the journey's effect. The feel of the tires on the road was intoxicating. And while I enjoyed jogging along the river, especially for the exercise, it was driving my car that provided the purest pleasure.

Big Sally and I were headed outbound, away from downtown. And I decided that if this was to be my last trip on East River Drive, I intended to enjoy it.

Once we passed the fountain at Sedgeley Road, with Boathouse Row to my left, I accelerated. Big Sally first voiced concern about our speed as we approached the Boathouse curve, a double-apex right-hander. The car bounced slightly as we went over the storm drains on the roadway. Just before the curve, I looked down at the speedometer. Fifty-five miles per hour.

The speed limit was thirty-five.

"Slow it down a bit," he said, the car's inertia forcing him to lean toward me as we curved to the right.

As I straightened the car, I checked to make sure my seatbelt was fastened tightly but said nothing to my passenger.

The gun in his right hand was his only protection against our increasing speed. His seatbelt wasn't fastened.

I took the curve to the left but there was traffic in both lanes in front of me. I darted into the lanes of on-coming traffic and passed the two cars before yanking the car back to the right and into my own lane. It was just before we passed under the Girard Street Bridge at more than sixty-five miles per hour.

"Damnit, I said slow down," Big Sally said, alarm inching into his voice.

One of the best parts of driving fast is having the wind in your hair. Selecting the button at my fingertips, I started with the driver side window, rolling it all the way down. Next came the window next to Big Sally, and then the windows in back. The roar of the cold wind through the windows made it hard for me to hear him, but I knew what he was saying.

Seventy miles per hour and accelerating as we approached Fountain Green Drive.

"What the fuck are you doin'?" Big Sally shouted, waving the gun around somewhat aimlessly.

"I like the air," I said.

"Slow down or I'll pop your ass right here and now."

"I doubt that. Not at this speed," I said as I opened the sunroof. Approaching seventy-five miles per hour. The lights on the cars heading in the opposite direction were becoming a blur.

Having the correct seat position is essential to efficiently operate any motor vehicle. Being able to reach the steering wheel without over-extending your arms, having the mirrors in the proper position for seeing, reaching the pedals without effort — all are important.

Not so much this time.

I pushed the seat back as far as it would go, making it harder to keep my right foot on the throttle. But I did. Seventy-eight, seventy-nine, eighty miles per hour.

And the idiot in the passenger seat was now facing me, banging his hand (which still held a gun) against the dashboard as he yelled. He was still unbuckled. If we crashed at that speed, he'd be thrown from the car. Not a good prospect for him.

The cold February air made the skin on my face tingle as it rushed in through the open windows.

"You fuckin' moron. Do you have a death wish?"

I didn't have a death wish but the likelihood of my dying had become apparent as soon as he walked into Allison's living room. Now, it was playing out on the East River Drive.

While I liked the Boathouse Curve, my favorite curve on the drive was the Grandstand Curve, so named because it was near the grandstands used for viewing the scull races on the river each spring and summer, the Dad Veil Regatta in May being the most famous. The Grandstand Curve had a decreasing radius and tightened up right at the apex, which was just as the road passed under a bridge.

Taking the curve at our speed — more than eighty miles per hour — would be challenging, if not impossible. And there was a storm drain just before the apex. Hitting it at eighty, assuming I made it that far into the turn, would almost certainly cause me to lose control and slam into the bridge abutment on the right or careen to the left and into on-coming traffic.

The options were to slow down or. . . .

I got the break I hoped for.

There were no on-coming cars as I approached the right-hand curve, so I yanked the steering wheel hard to the left. I crossed the two left lanes and the car bucked violently as it went over the curb and crossed a narrow bicycle path. I think one of the tires blew out and the car slowed somewhat as my foot briefly slipped off the throttle. But we were still headed across the grass at a considerable speed straight for a wall that dropped off into the dark, murky waters of the Schuylkill River. It was less than one hundred feet away — and fast approaching.

"I'm going to fuckin' kill you," Big Sally shouted, staring forward at the looming river's edge. He extended both arms to the dashboard to brace himself for an accident he could do nothing to prevent.

A watery death was coming for us both, but I certainly preferred it to Salvatore Ricci forcing me to dig a grave for Benito "the Baker" Patrese and then shooting me.

I tugged once more on my seatbelt to see if it was secure. I doubted Big Sally heard me say under my breath, "I hope you can swim."

CHAPTER XXIV

The water was a muddy brown —
and mind-numbingly cold.

The car flew out over the water and seemed to hang there in the air. But then, the inevitable.

The nose of the car, which is the heaviest part of the vehicle because it housed the engine, dipped and the water seemed to reach up and grab us, pulling us straight down. When the car hit the river, water splashed upward and in every direction. The sudden deceleration caused the unbelted Big Sally to pitch violently forward. His hands against the dashboard were not nearly enough protection and he slammed headfirst into the windshield, cracking the window.

And probably his head.

I was more fortunate. Though wrenched forward, the seatbelt kept me from being impaled by the steering wheel.

Because of the angle and speed at which the car hit the water, the front of the car instantly submerged up to the windshield. Water was coming in from every opening, through the floor, the dashboard, the steering wheel column and all the heating and air-conditioning vents. And within seconds, through the open front windows, too. We were sinking fast.

The water was a muddy brown — and mind-numbingly cold.

I had never felt water that cold before and it jolted my senses. It didn't appear to have the same effect on Big Sally, who had fallen back into his seat as the rear of the car settled. He was either unconscious or completely dazed. I couldn't tell which in the darkness.

But Big Sally wasn't my main concern. In fact, he was barely a concern at all. My priority was to get out of the car before it totally submerged.

I reached down with my right hand and released the seatbelt, pulling it away from my body with my left hand. The water was already up to my stomach. Big Sally, still dazed, was falling in my direction, forced by the water flooding through his window. I pushed him over and pulled myself up and out of the seat. The water was up to my chest.

The river seemed to suck me down. But I finally stood up in the seat and used the edges of the sunroof to hoist myself up through the opening. Nearly the entire interior of the car was under water by then and the car was still sinking. Once on the roof, I jumped into the darkened water and started swimming toward the water's edge. I spit water out of my mouth with each stroke.

The river didn't taste any better than it looked.

I didn't look back until I reached the slippery, wet, weather-worn brick wall that separated the river from the land. The water bubbled as the car continued its journey down, and it finally disappeared under the surface. The last of the car to go was the trunk, which carried the already dead body of Benito "the Baker" Patrese on the way to a watery grave.

It was difficult getting a hold on the slippery brick wall, which was a worry until a pair of passersby — a guy and his date — who must have witnessed the accident, stopped their vehicle and rushed to my aid. Both reached down to grab my arms and hauled me out of the water and over to a nearby bench.

"What happened, man?" the guy asked as he put his dry jacket over my wet shoulders and started to rub my arms to improve circulation. "Rachel, go call the cops."

"How? There's no payphone out here," she replied.

I looked over toward the water but didn't see anyone else come out.

~*~

I was sitting on the back of a boxy, red-and-white emergency response vehicle, wrapped in a thick, heavy blanket with Philadelphia Fire Department printed on the back when Thompson walked into my line of sight. I was still shaking from the cold and warming my hands on the outside of a hot cup of coffee. I wished I had on dry clothes. I doubted I'd ever be warm again.

East River Drive was blocked off in both directions and the red-and-blue flashing lights of what seemed like hundreds of police cars and fire trucks gave the scene an eerie quality. Seemed like every officer in the city was at the accident scene.

About forty feet away, a gaggle of police officers interviewed the couple who had fished me out of the water. They didn't know that two others were in the car when it went in. I didn't mention that to them.

Thompson just stood for a moment looking down at me, shaking his head. "What in the world were you thinking, David?"

"Well, hello to you, too," I said, waiting a heartbeat for a response that wasn't coming before I answered the question as best I could. "It seemed like a good idea at the time."

Taking another sip of the strong black coffee, I looked over toward the river. Powerful search lights were shining out onto the water in the direction of where the car disappeared. "Where's your partner, O'Donnell?"

"We're off duty tonight?"

"Then why are you here?"

"I always get a call when something happens involving you because you're a person-of-interest in a murder case. Seem to get a lot of calls lately," he said. "What happened?"

"Salvatore Ricci was going to have me dig a grave for his father-in-law, Benito Patrese, and then shoot me. Patrese's body's in the trunk of the car. I didn't want to get shot, so I drove the car into the river," I said, putting the coffee down and rubbing my hands together. "They find any bodies?"

"Too dark. Divers will get here in the morning. First thing," he said.

"Ricci was still in the front passenger seat when I got out of the car."

"Dead?"

"I don't know," I said. "The gun that probably killed Patrese and was used to kill Henry Cummings is with Patrese's body in the trunk. I think Ricci did it."

"Why?"

"He and Allison Charles, the city economic development director, were in league together. They're trying to consolidate gambling and other illegal activities throughout the city."

"Ricci I can see. But why Allison Charles?" Thompson asked. "I don't get that."

"Henry Cummings was her uncle and she's now running his illegal numbers operation in North Philly. But no one knows that. She and Ricci were planning to pick up the pieces after Patrese and DelMarco killed each other in their mob war. Then they'd control most of the organized crime in north AND south Philly."

"You got proof? Can't do much without some proof."

"I was at her house tonight. She told me," I said.

"Still, her word against yours," he said. "And why would she tell you that?"

"Because she thought I'd be dead by now."

"But you aren't," he said, shaking his head in disbelief. "And she'll deny everything you've just told me, of course."

"Yes. But I got the proof . . . a paper trail . . . and sent it to you by mail for safe keeping. You should have it by tomorrow," I said.

"I talked to the emergency guys. They say you can go home. Once again, who do I need to call?"

"My sister and brother-in-law," I said.

"I seem to be calling them a lot. Let's see if I can do less of that in the future, okay, David?"

"You guys gonna talk to Allison Charles?"

"Tomorrow. If what you say checks out, she could be behind bars by the afternoon."

~*~

My sopping wet clothes and shoes were in a pile on the bathroom floor, as was the towel I used to dry off, when I came out wearing sweatpants and sweatshirt. I was dry but still felt cold.

It was after three in the morning and Valerie and Stuart were standing by the front door in my living room.

"Here. Take this," Valerie said, handing me a red Temple University mug containing a warm, dark liquid. "It's hot tea. It's good for you. Drink it."

I hugged Valerie, then pulled away to see her more fully. "Thanks again for everything. I appreciate it."

"We ready?" Stuart said, clearly impatient to go home. "It's late."

"Make sure to call Clara tonight, and I'll call Grammy Taylor in the morning," Valerie said.

"I'll call as soon as you guys are out the door. I promise."

"Is it all over? Your investigation?" Stuart asked, taking my hand as they prepared to leave. His palms were wet. Mine were not.

"I think so, yes."

He looked relieved. Valerie just looked tired.

"Get some sleep," she said, kissing my cheek one last time, and they were out the door.

I didn't want to call Clara and wake her, but I knew it was the best thing. I may be a horrible boyfriend but certainly not a dreadful one. And as for being a horrible grandson, I would have to wait until morning to discover that.

With Valerie and Stuart gone, I was alone in the darkened apartment and, surprisingly, felt warm for the first time in what seemed like hours. The telephone beside my bed beckoned me. I knew what I needed to do but hesitated. Clara hated my job, and all the time it took me to find paying gigs and then the long hours it took doing the work. But she was comforted by the fact that most of my cases weren't especially dangerous.

Nearly getting assassinated by a clown and now this — driving a car into the Schuylkill to escape a mobster — might be more than she could handle.

As I sat on the bed thinking about the call, exhaustion pulled me down and I knew if I waited any longer, I'd fall asleep. I picked up the phone and dialed.

She answered on the second ring.

"Hello?" she said, sleep heavy in her voice.

"It's David. Sorry to wake you."

"Are you all right, David?" she said. I heard alarm creeping into her voice.

"I'm fine, I'm fine," I assured her, pausing for a couple of heartbeats before continuing. "But there was an accident tonight. And I think we need to talk."

~*~

The telephone beside the bed rang at an insanely early hour in the morning and I was asked to come down to the police station. I showered and lingered under the hot water, drenching myself from head to toe. It felt inviting. I never again wanted to feel water as cold as that in the Schuylkill River in the wintertime.

At the station I gave my official statement and was introduced to an assistant district attorney, Millicent Hawkins, who was handling the case. Detectives went to visit Allison. After being questioned, she was told not to leave the city.

"Have you seen today's early edition of the Daily News?" Hawkins asked.

I replied no, and she pulled a copy out of her briefcase

and laid it on the desk in front of me. The picture was of the car, water pouring out of its windows, as a crane lifted it out of the river. The headline over Georgios Aristidis' byline read:

Two Mobsters Dead Inside

"Story's on Page 3. It's their lead story. Quotes some anonymous city sources. No telling who that may be," she said, smiling and raising an eyebrow as she walked off.

I read the story.

> Philadelphia police divers early today pulled a maroon Honda out of the Schuylkill River that reportedly held the bodies of two reputed mob figures and a gun possibly linked to the murder of a major numbers runner on the city's northside, law enforcement officials say.
>
> The names of the two men pulled from the car were not being released, pending notification of next of kin, a police spokeswoman said. However, a law enforcement source close to the investigation said the victims were reputed mob boss Benito Patrese and his underboss, Salvatore Ricci.
>
> The source asked not to be named because they were not authorized to speak to the press.
>
> One body was found in the car's trunk, while one was in the car's front passenger seat. An autopsy is scheduled to determine the manner and cause of death of both men, though the passenger was believed to have drowned.
>
> The car went into the river on East River Drive near the Grandstand Curve at around 11:30 last night, said police spokesman Judy Hennessy. The car matched the description of a Honda police were looking for in connection with a fatal hit-and-run accident earlier this week.
>
> "The car was being driven by a local private

detective at the time [of the accident last night]. We have not released his name. We are not sure where the car was going or why it veered off the road and into the river," Hennessy said. "We are still looking to determine those facts. The investigation is ongoing."

The private detective driving the car was later identified as David Blaise, 32, of West Philadelphia. Blaise, who swam ashore after the Honda went into the water, was apparently unharmed in the accident. He has not been charged with a crime and is helping with the investigation, officials said.

Calls to Blaise's North Philadelphia office were unanswered this morning.

The gun found in the car was reportedly linked to the shooting death of Henry Cummings in a townhouse in Queen Village two weeks ago, sources said. Cummings operated an illegal gambling empire out of a gas station at Broad and Caleb in North Philadelphia.

The Honda was linked to the hit-and-run death of Marion "Chuckie" Johnson this week outside the gas station owned by Cummings.

Patrese, also known as "Benito the Baker," was reportedly involved in a bloody feud with mob rival Michele "Mikie" DelMarco for control of organized crime in the Philadelphia/South Jersey area. Nearly two dozen murders have been linked to Mafia feuds since the assassination four years ago of mob boss Angelo Bruno.

Law enforcement officials were unsure of the connection between the on-going mob war and Cummings' death.

Incidentally, the U.S. Attorney's Office for the Eastern District of Pennsylvania this afternoon is set to indict Patrese, DelMarco and 12 other mob associates with racketeering, said federal officials, who asked not to be named. Among the charges in the 213-count indictment are murder, extortion, illegal gambling, prostitution, drug distribution, and loan sharking.

The federal charges stem from an investigation dating back more than a year and are unrelated to this morning's incident, officials said. At least 12 murders are directly linked to the federal charges.

O'Donnell and Thompson were coming over by the time I finished reading.

"Looks like some good public relations for you, Blaise, having your name in the paper on a major story," O'Donnell said, taking a chair at the next desk.

"Johnny, leave the man alone. He had a rough time last night," Thompson said.

I got up and was about to start for the door. "I'm gone, unless you guys need me for anything else. I'm headed up to my office to close out another case. Then I'm going to lunch."

I left the station and reached my office thirty minutes later. I walked in and sat down in a chair directly in front of Larry's desk.

"Man, I'm tired. It was a long night. A really long night."

"I read about it in the papers. Your phone's been ringing off the hook and people . . . reporters mostly . . . have been stopping by all morning," he said. "I just tell them I have no idea where you are. Vipers, the lot of them."

I laughed. "I didn't see anyone outside."

"You're lucky. What were you doing in that car, anyway?"

"It's a long story but right now, I'm hungry. Feels like days since I've had food. You want to get something to eat? I'm paying. And I'll tell you all about it over a meal," I said.

"You solve my case?"

"Yes, I have. I'm sending you the invoice this afternoon. It's why I can afford to pay for lunch."

"Tell me about it," Centerton said.

"We can do it over lunch. That and much more," I said.

Centerton looked around his office and finally placed his hands on his considerable stomach. "Then I'll pay," he said. "Where to? I don't want to walk far."

"I'd like some seafood. How about The Frog restaurant downtown? Eighteenth and Sansom, right on the corner. I'll drive."

We got in the Mustang and made mindless conversation on the way to Center City. I parked in a garage on Sansom a half a block from the restaurant, so it was a short walk for Centerton, who, nevertheless, was breathing heavily by the time we arrived. The man needed to lose some weight and I imagined that might be happening soon.

The lunchtime rush was in full swing and we had to wait about five minutes before we got a table, which was near the back. But that was okay with me.

It was a two-top and we sat across from each other, with me facing the front.

"Tell me about last night," he said once we were settled in at a table. There were occupied tables on either side of us and I was sure other patrons could hear our conversation as easily as we heard theirs.

"You read the newspaper. Not that much to tell, except that one of those guys was holding a gun to me. The river was my only choice, which is why we went in," I said. Out of the side of my eye, I noticed the gentleman next to me taking notice. He tried to discreetly glance my way while he ate. "I was lucky to get out of it alive."

"I'll say," my obese guest said, before impatiently adding, "But my case. What about my case?"

"Let's order first," I said.

Centerton said nothing as the waiter arrived and I thanked him when he handed us menus. "Specials?" I asked.

He ran through a list for today and departed after taking our drink orders, promising to return shortly to take our lunch orders.

"You wanted to come here. What's good?" Centerton said, placing his napkin across his massive lap.

"Crab bisque," I said but, as I looked over the top of my menu, I added, "Though you might want to order yours To Go."

"What? To Go? Good heavens why? We just got here."

Thompson, O'Donnell and two men in dark suits whom I didn't recognize approached the table.

"Larry Centerton?" said one of the dark suits, the taller of the two.

"Yes," Centerton said, looking around, puzzled. "Who are you?"

I answered before any of them had a chance.

"These two gentlemen here . . . Thompson and O'Donnell . . . are Philadelphia police officers, though I'm not altogether sure why they're here," I said, starting with the introductions. "These other two look like G-men, am I right? You're FBI?"

Now we had the attention of both the tables on either side of us. And they weren't trying to hide it.

"FBI Special Agent Pearson and Special Agent Brown," Pearson said, removing his ID and flipping it open for Centerton to see. "Please stand up and place your arms behind your back. You are under arrest for theft and embezzlement."

The agents lifted him from his seat and Centerton grimaced when they tightened the handcuffs behind his back.

"You have the right to remain silent," the agent continued. "Anything you say may and will be held against you in a court of law. You have the right to have an attorney present during questioning. If you do not have the money for an attorney, the court can appoint an attorney to represent you. Do you understand?"

Centerton was struck nearly speechless and, being totally confused, merely nodded. Now, all the people in the restaurant were staring. This wasn't a regular occurrence at The Frog.

I looked up at Centerton and got his attention just as they were about to take him away.

"It wasn't your partner who was stealing money from the firm. It was you, Larry. If you didn't want me to figure that out, you shouldn't have hired me."

Though he should have remained silent, Centerton spoke up.

"Leslie was getting suspicious, so I got the jump on him by hiring you. I didn't think you'd find much and if you did, you couldn't tell anyone. It would be privileged information that was between only us two," he said.

"That's stupid, Larry. Such privilege doesn't extend to illegal information. I could go to jail. We both would. I discovered the second set of accounting books you kept and, after I contacted the bank about your finances, they found your secret bank accounts," I said.

"Let's go," one of the agents said, pulling Centerton away from the table. But he was still facing me, horror playing across his face. The flab under his double chin jiggled, though I wasn't sure if it was from anger or fear.

"Guess this means you aren't paying me," I said as Centerton was finally turned toward the door and headed out with the two federal agents. "I could still use the money," I added softly, mostly to myself.

"Good job, Mr. Detective," O'Donnell said. "He's also going to be charged locally. That's why we came along. We'll catch up with you later."

"Yeah, I'm still going to have lunch," I said.

"I think I'll do the same, in a little while," O'Donnell said as they were about to leave. "Anything good up your way?"

"Don't know what you like. You'll just have to come up and see," I said as the officers turned and left.

The waiter returned, somewhat surprised at what had just happened. Uncertain, he said, "Would you. . . ."

"Yes, I'd like to order. And I'll start with the crab bisque."

CHAPTER XXV

"I feel honored."

After a relatively expensive lunch, which I couldn't afford, because my paying client had just been arrested, and after solving several cases on the same day, I was back in the office in the afternoon. I would have to move into the new office, of course. Lucky for me, I didn't have that much to pack, but I would still need help getting things up to my new digs in West Philadelphia. I'd have more space and it would cost me less than what I was paying for the back office of an accounting firm in North Philadelphia. Handling Stuart's problem without the family catching on proved to be a blessing, although I wasn't sure what it would be like to have him as a landlord.

I worked packing my desk and putting my files in boxes. I opened the bottom drawer on the right and pulled out my gun, leaving it on the desk as I continued.

Fifteen minutes later, I heard the front door to the accounting office open and into my office walked Officer O'Donnell.

"I thought I'd come up here on my lunchtime, but I'm in a bit of a rush so I can't eat," he said. His right hand was on the butt of his gun, which, while still holstered, was quickly and easily accessible.

I was sitting but took a quick look at my gun only inches away to my right. He saw that, too.

"Don't try it. I don't want to kill you here, but I will if you move," he said. "Now get up. Slowly."

"Why? You're going to kill me either way," I said.

"True. But not here . . . unless I must."

"How many has it been? Assassinations, I mean."

O'Donnell glanced around quickly as if counting them up in his head. But his attention was never fully off me or the gun on the desk.

"Since I was made? Nine. Nine in all. You'll make ten."

"I feel honored."

"You should be."

"Were you in or out of uniform? The killings, that is. Before you became a police officer."

"A little of both."

"Impressive, considering. I just wanted to know."

"Well, now you do," he said, pulling out his gun. "I said get up."

I remained still. "Once you use that, they'll know it's you. You won't be able to use that gun again, and you'll have to explain what happened to it," I said. "But it doesn't matter. They're on to you already."

"Think so, huh? I doubt it. Big Sally's dead, so he can't talk. And Allison knows what's good for her. She'll keep her mouth shut and if not, she'll finger Big Sally. And that will be it," he said.

"If you kill me, you could face the death penalty in Pennsylvania. Let me go and turn yourself in, and you might be able to strike a deal to save your life. You'll spend the rest of it in prison, of course, but you'd be alive. And who knows, maybe some judge in forty years might take pity on you and let you out if you've been a good boy for all that time."

"Don't be stupid," he said with a sneer. But then he looked uncertain. "What are you talking about?"

"I knew there was a leak in the department but I wasn't sure about you until you told me to have a nice time in Atlantic City. That was the dead giveaway . . . pardon the pun. I hadn't told you about Atlantic City, only that I was going away for the weekend. I hadn't told anyone except Clara. But Big Sally overheard me on the phone. He knew. He told you, so you knew," I said. "What is he to you, anyway? You can't be brothers. The department would have uncovered that."

He looked at me with a growing hatred. It surprised me that someone who had dedicated his life to killing people and covering it up could be so easily riled.

"Distant cousins. On my mother's side," he said. "Different last names."

"Ah, yes. I see now. You're the cousin Big Sally mentioned to me. Giovanni. Italian for Johnny," I said. "The city needs to do a better job of vetting applicants. You and Allison are fine examples of that."

"It's not going to be a concern for you for very long. Now get up," he said, anger rising in his voice.

"It's a funny thing," I said, waving my pointer finger over my head toward the upper walls. "You're being recorded right now. I hope you know that. The department bugged my office after Benito Patrese was here. Well, at least I think it was the Philadelphia Police Department."

I pointed to the air vent on the wall near the ceiling. "From up there, you get a totally unobstructed view of the entire office. Of me and you. That's where they put the camera. There's a microphone in the lamp here and likely a bug in the mouthpiece of the phone. I haven't looked, because I didn't want them to know I was on to them.

"I was in Naval intelligence in the military and handled a lot of signal intelligence. I'm familiar with all sorts of eavesdropping equipment. Comes in handy in my current line of work. I'd imagine the local feds can get the same stuff we had in the military. This stuff isn't as good, sorry to say. It's why I thought it was the local cops who planted it. I noticed it immediately.

"And I've already sent your department your bank withdrawal records. They have a security camera shot of Big

Sally making a deposit at a PSFS branch on Passyunk and later in the day a shot of you withdrawing cash from a Center City branch on Walnut. I'm sorry, but you're done. You're going to prison."

O'Donnell looked like he was ready to shoot me in the office.

"Put the gun down, Johnny! *Now*!" Thompson said, rushing in through the front door, followed by more than a half dozen heavily armed police officers. "Don't make me shoot you. I will, and you know it. Don't make me."

O'Donnell looked at me and then back to Thompson. He dropped his gun.

"You are under arrest for murder, extortion and a host of other charges," Thompson said to O'Donnell. To the men behind him, he instructed, "Read him his rights and get him out of here." He shoved O'Donnell in the direction of the front door.

I sat down again and looked around. I wasn't going to miss this office. "What took you so long?"

"We were a little busy. We took Allison Charles into custody. Charged her with murder and an assortment of other offenses," Thompson said. "Had to take care of that first." Then, in a nearly light-hearted way, he added, "And do you have any idea of how many traffic lights there are between here and City Hall?"

I just shook my head in disbelief.

"It's quite a lot," he said.

"And you couldn't put on your flashers?" I asked, half seriously, half not.

"Your office is bugged. Mostly just for recording, but there's a transmitter to get a live signal."

"I thought as much," I said. "Makes sense."

"I was listening all the way up here," he said with a smile, putting his left hand on my shoulder as he stuck out his right hand. "Take care of yourself, David."

We shook.

"You, too, John," I said, slowly adding. "You, too."

CHAPTER XXVI

The dead waited for no one.

It wasn't Sunday night, but I needed the comfort of family. It had been a hard couple of weeks and the best remedy was a visit to my grandmother's house. When I got there, she was preparing to go to a wake. I can't imagine how she went to all those wakes and funerals without becoming suicidal, but she managed quite well.

She didn't know the deceased; they were a distant relative of one of her friends, and Grammy Taylor would go to support them.

"How in the world are you even getting there?" I asked as I sat at the foot of her bed. She was standing in front of her vanity, adjusting a black hat she was about to pin into place. She had on a black and fuchsia herringbone suit with a black blouse, which was one of the outfits she wore to such occasions. I really liked the outfit. It was totally right — somber, because of the black, but without being maudlin, because of the fuchsia.

And it was appropriate for her age and figure.

"Midge's son is driving us," she said. She looked at my reflection in the mirror and turned back to me. "Davey, life is hard. Relationships are hard. But you do good work, helping people like your sister," Grammy Taylor said.

"Helping her how?"

"You know . . . when you helped Stuart with his problem," she said, turning back to the mirror, no longer looking at me. She adjusted the hat and eased a long, straight hat pin into it, thus holding it in place. "In that way, you helped Valerie." Grammy turned back to me. "I don't care for him . . . you know that . . . but she does. That should be enough."

The depth of her love of family was palpable. She obviously knew something about Stuart and had kept it secret from the rest of us, including me. My admiration for the woman grew. She was amazing.

Without saying another word, Grammy Taylor picked up a pair of black gloves and a black purse that were sitting on the bed next to me and walked downstairs.

The dead waited for no one.

About the Author

Photo by Jay Alley

MB Dabney is an award-winning retired journalist with numerous short-story titles to his name. His debut novel, AN UNTIDY AFFAIR, was praised as a "gripping mystery" and a "roller-coaster ride" with a surprising and satisfying ending. He is the father of two adult daughters and lives in Indiana with his wife, Angela.

Also Praise for An Untidy Affair

"Dabney has created one of the smartest, toughest, funniest private investigators in today's PI fiction."

Susan Furlong, *Shattered Justice*, A New York Times Top Ten Crime Novel

"This murder mystery/thriller takes readers on a real emotional roller coaster with twists and unusually surprising turns — all against a vivid Philadelphia backdrop. The descriptive writing brings all the characters, their suspenseful actions and Philly's streets to life."

The Philadelphia Tribune

"Protagonist David Blaise is the type of PI Easy Rawlins or Sam Spade would buy a beer and trade war stories (with) on a warm summer night. Great read, great mystery."

Robin Lee Lovelace, author of the award-winning novella *Savonne, Not Vonny*.